The PARALLEL UNIVERSE of LIARS

Kathleen Jeffrie
JOHNSON

Published by
Dell Laurel-Leaf
an imprint of
Random House Children's Books
a division of Random House, Inc.
New York

Visit us on the Web! www.randomhouse.com/teens

Educators and librarians, for a variety of teaching tools,
visit us at
www.randomhouse.com/teachers

ISBN: 0-440-23852-8

RL: 6.0

Reprinted by arrangement with Roaring Brook Press

Printed in the United States of America

March 2004

10 9 8 7 6 5 4 3 2 1

OPM

How can we light our way into the dark
If not by human love?

For those who have helped me light my way

One

Nobody ever tells you what to do when you're hopeless and fat and your only friend is moving to Alabama.

"You'll make new friends," Mother says, leaning toward the mirror to stroke mascara on her lashes, darkening them perfectly.

I don't want to make new friends. I want to keep the one I have—Melissa. In a couple of weeks, she'll be gone.

"When you lose a few pounds," Mother adds, twisting the mascara shut, "your social life will perk right up." She turns in her chair and smiles at me, touching my cheek with her fingertips. Last night she changed her polish from Apricot Angel to Ruby Rush, so now her nails are flaming red. "Just follow the diet the doctor is going to give you, honey." She opens her matching tube of Ruby Rush lipstick and glides it over her lips. "It comes down to willpower."

Even if I *did* lose weight, I'd still never look like Mother. I take after Dad—short and shaped like a pear.

Mother's blond and a lot taller than me, plus she's got these hooters. She's even had a face lift. So though she's really old—fifty-four—she always manages to find a boyfriend.

She blots excess lipstick off her mouth and stands up.

"I'm glad I went with the navy blue," she says. "I think Dick will like it." If he likes his girlfriend in a short dress with a snug fit and white piping, he'll be happy.

I don't have anything to show off. My tummy sticks out farther than my breasts.

Yesterday, Frankie, my next-door neighbor, patted my stomach and said, "What's that you got in there, babe, a plateful of biscuits?" Then he laughed and turned back to his full-length mirror to study himself again. He had a hot date with China, and he likes to look just right. He's twenty-three; his stomach is hard and flat, and he's so good-looking he's a part-time model and actor. He works as a bartender at Raze, in D.C., to fill in the space between gigs, but he expects to be famous soon.

People like that should not make fun of other people's stomachs.

Mother turns back to the mirror for one last check, smoothing the corners of her lips with her pinky. "I think Dick's gonna be my lucky guy!" She means she thinks she can get him to marry her.

I've never had a live-in dad.

Frankie's mom has three snake plants, twenty-two African violets, one Norfolk Island pine, two maidenhair ferns, five bougainvilleas, four tiny cacti, plus a whole bunch of other plants, including one with pink speckles:

forty-seven houseplants altogether. Since Frankie either drowns them or lets them parch, Mrs. Jenkins hires me to water them when she's out of town on business, which is just about all the time—she's a sales rep for Greater Soaps and Deodorants.

I always worry I'm going to kill everything—naturally, all the plants get thirsty at different times—but so far I haven't. Mrs. Jenkins pays me pretty good so I try to be careful. She even gave me a key to their house.

I go in the living room and tip the little plastic watering can, giving the first bougainvillea a drink.

This is actually my second job. Three times a week I volunteer for a couple of hours at Collingsdale Nursing Home. I read to the residents or help them eat their lunch. Mother signed me up for the summer. She says it will help build my character. I'd rather just build my bank account.

I finish up the bougainvillea and empty the watering can into Mrs. Jenkins's kitchen sink. Some days the plants seem depressed or something, but today everybody's okay. So am I. Who cares if my doctor's appointment is this afternoon? I'm wearing my favorite red shorts, and they still fit! So take that, Dr. Fat Finder. Plus my birthday's in one week and one day: Saturday, July 30. I'll be fifteen.

I head out the front door.

"Hey, Robin." Frankie's washing his Ford Probe—red, with double-line black racing stripes running front to back over the roof. He expects his car to be as good-looking as he is.

"You got a job this weekend?" I ask. He's got that *hot* look about him, like all his chromosomes are concentrating extra hard on being handsome.

He squeezes out a giant sponge, getting his cutoffs even wetter than they already are. His chest is bare and tan. "An acting gig, babe. Host at this seafood festival, boat show thing, over in Ocean Side."

That's three hours away from here, on the other side of Maryland. We live on *this* side of Maryland, right outside of Washington, D.C. The boring side—unless you like C-SPAN and politics.

He winks at me and picks up the hose. "Just me and my bikini."

"Oh." I see him in his bikini all the time—he does his sunning in the backyard—so I know he'll be one of the highlights of the festival. "Just you?"

"Me and a whole bunch of chicks and a few other guys." He rinses suds off the top of his car. "Plus all these geezers, chowing down crab cakes and beer, thinking *sex on a boat with a babe!* It's my job to hot up the wives." He laughs. "Let me tell you, the wallets will open." He crouches down to get the left front tire.

It's hard not to watch. His official description is: "Six feet two, slender but muscled, with dark hair and deep blue eyes. *Handsome.*" That's how his agent describes him. That's how he describes himself, especially on a good mirror day. On a good mirror day, he grins and rearranges the miniature furniture in his mother's handmade Victorian dollhouse, maybe putting the bathtub in the attic or sliding the bitsy footstools down the banister. On a *bad* mirror day, he frowns and bangs the side of the dollhouse on his way out the door, making all the tiny chests tip over and the chandeliers shake.

It's always back in order, though, before his mother comes home.

He's been working out with weights for a while now, so his chest is a lot better than it used to be, and so are his legs. I guess his body is just about perfect, but mostly he's got this *face.* It's the kind of face that sucks all the air out of a room, that makes your mouth drop open. His nose is fine and straight, and his lips have this curve in them that makes people sweat. That's what his agent says. Frankie's lips are one of his selling points.

I stand in the wet grass beside the driveway, wearing my red shorts and white T-shirt. Mother says red makes me look fat, but maybe it makes me look *hot,* like Frankie's car. Red's supposed to be a sexy color.

I wait for him to finish the tire and stand up. He brings me stuff back from his jobs, like a Z-Man T-shirt or a Waster baseball cap, and once he gave me a shiny pink Forever gift bag full of perfumes and makeup. Maybe this time he'll bring me a box of saltwater taffy.

I watch the curve of his back as he rinses, the way his rear end is outlined in his shorts. If I lose weight, maybe *my* rear end will be somebody's highlight. So far, the only one who's noticed it is old Mr. Simmons at the nursing home. He keeps trying to pinch me on the fanny.

I see that Frankie has dropped the big sponge on the ground, so I bend over to pick it up.

Smack! Water hits me right in the rear end.

"Hey," he laughs. "It's little Robin red butt!"

I turn and throw the sponge at him and run home, slamming the kitchen door behind me.

In my bedroom I pull off my shorts and dump them in the trash. I stand in my wet underpants, breathing hard. Peeling off my underwear, I turn and look in the mirror. Little Robin fat butt.

* * *

Melissa likes orange Popsicles best. They almost match the color of her curly, orangey-red hair. Sort of. Me, I'm a purple girl. Of course, I'd prefer a Nutsie Boy cone, but Mother would kill me if she caught me eating one. Melissa's so tall and skinny she could eat a hundred Nutsie Boy cones and never gain weight. She's the only one I know who has never, in one way or another, let me know I'm fat.

I sit on the front step, finishing a purple, waiting for Mother to come home from work to take me to my doctor's appointment. I'm wearing slacks now, even though it's eighty-seven degrees out—I don't want anyone else looking at my rear end. Frankie's car is still in his driveway, shiny and clean. I unwrap my second purple just as Mother pulls up.

"Honestly, Robin," she says, when I get in the car. She thinks I'm too old and fat for Popsicles, but I don't really see how there can be an age limit. I think you can still eat them if you're almost fifteen. It's not like there's a law that says you get arrested if you weigh too much and are caught with a purple tongue. Besides, a Popsicle has a lot less calories than a Nutsie Boy.

Frankie comes out of his house wearing jeans and a T-shirt. He throws a small piece of luggage in the back of his car, then waves at us before getting in the front seat. Mother and I wave back, watching as he adjusts the rearview mirror.

My Popsicle starts melting.

"Look at him," Mother sighs. She's got that wistful tone in her voice that she gets whenever she looks at him. "He's enough to make your teeth ache."

She waits for him to pull out of his driveway, then follows him down the road all the way to the highway. When he turns right to get to the Beltway, we turn left. He sticks his arm out the window to wave good-bye.

"When you lose weight," Mother says, "you'll find yourself a boyfriend in no time." She glances at herself in the rearview mirror. "Just like China."

Frankie used to date a different girl every night, but once he met China, that was it. She's an actress, too, in between classes at the University of Maryland. She's got a pretty face and wavy, honey-blond hair, the kind that's long and thick and shiny, plus a tiny waist and major breasts. Frankie says they're all hers. She got a bit part in a Wally's Sport and Spa commercial—a steady shot of her cleavage as she works out. Together, she and Frankie are *hot.* That's what he says, winking. *Hot.*

"You'll get a boy soon," says Mother.

I chomp down on my Popsicle. All I've got is Mr. Simmons. He's *way* too old to be called a boy, plus he's disgusting.

Mother tried to get me ready for a boyfriend three years ago, when I turned twelve. She handed me my present, a big boxed set of Bad Girl makeup. It had everything—eye shadows, lipsticks, mascara, powder.

My best feature is my eyes. They're big and wide, a light blue-gray. "See, everybody has at least one asset," she said. We were sitting in front of her vanity table, looking at ourselves in the mirror. She opened the Bad Girl makeup box and pulled out a mascara. My eyelashes are light brown, lighter than my hair, which is medium brown. "You just need to make your lashes darker." She handed me the mascara wand, and I leaned in toward the mirror—and poked myself right in the eye. It burned like crazy, sending tears streaking down my cheek. I haven't tried it since.

I've got all the edges of my paper gown tamped down so nothing shows, but the doctor immediately pulls everything open and slaps a stethoscope right next to my left breast. I feel like a naked piggy.

I have to breathe in deeply and exhale. He listens; then I have to do it again.

"I know I'm fat," I say, hoping he'll stop.

He starts poking and prodding around, pausing when he discovers my purple tongue. "Bubble gum?" he asks, holding it down with a tongue depressor. I shake my head no. "Popsicle?" I nod, trying not to gag, and he releases it and charges ahead, peering into my eyeballs and up my nose. I really think the inside of your nose is nobody else's business. "Get dressed," he finally says.

I sit with Mother in his office as he sighs and frowns, flipping through my records. He clears his throat. "Well, you certainly could lose a good twenty pounds. You don't want to get any heavier."

Mother smiles. "I think a strict diet—"

He ignores Mother and looks at me over his glasses. "Watch the desserts, eat lots of fruit and vegetables, and get plenty of exercise. Come back in six months and we'll see how you're doing."

Mother's smile disappears.

We stop at Super Food on the way home. Mother loads bags of carrots and celery and all kinds of fruit into the grocery cart. While she's back in Meats, I sneak into the express line and buy a Milky Way. I've got all summer to lose weight.

I check the plants next door while Mother's watching *60 Minutes.* I watch it with her sometimes, since there's not a whole lot to do on Sunday night, but it's mostly boring. It should be called *Stinky Minutes.*

Cacti go forever without wanting any water, but then they want some—you just don't know *when.* So once a week I give them a tiny sip, just in case. It's frustrating that I can't really communicate with them.

I hear a car and a minute later Frankie walks in. What's he doing home so early? He wasn't due back till tomorrow.

"Hey, babe," he says, tossing his gear on a chair. He has his own apartment downstairs, but he still strews stuff all over the place upstairs.

I set the watering can down. "What did you bring me?" I ask.

He laughs, smelling faintly of beer and sunscreen. "Hold on a minute, would you?" He pulls open a small cooler and hands me a plastic container, wet from sitting on ice. I open it. "A Genuine Ocean Side Seafood Festival/Boat Show Crab Cake," he says. "The *best.*" It's got a little tub of coleslaw with it. I break off a piece as he heads into the kitchen. It tastes good, spicy and sweet, fleshy—not exactly like meat but not exactly like fish. I follow him into the kitchen.

"How was the boat show?"

"Great," he says, downing a big glass of water. "It

ended early because a storm blew up. But before that—" He winks at me over his glass. "Met a ton of chicks, babe. We were *burning*. I made it with two of them. Man, talk about happy!"

The crab cake sticks in my throat. He *made* it with them? What about China?

He swallows and sets the glass down, wiping his mouth on his arm. "That's between you and me, okay?" He smacks me on the rear end on his way out of the kitchen. I hear his feet thump down the steps to his apartment.

"Okay." I set the rest of the crab cake on the counter and go home.

At the nursing home today, Mrs. Henley—who's got more wrinkles than a road map and drools—snorted her apple juice up through her nose. It was disgusting. I will never drink apple juice when I'm old, and I certainly won't expect an innocent teenager to clean me up afterward.

I sit down on the side step, unwrap a purple Popsicle, and chomp. Fortunately, Popsicles cannot be snorted.

Just as I get it down to a few lines of purple ice, the kitchen door opens and Mother steps out. She's wearing her lime green dress, the one I found for her at Maxim's department store, running back and forth between the fitting room and the dress racks, bringing her skirts and dresses and blouses to try on. She and Dick have a major date tonight. Their relationship is heating up.

She glares at my Popsicle. I only have a couple of scrapes left. I start scraping.

The lime somehow doesn't clash with her hair, which is freshly streaked and really bright, like the beacon in a lighthouse. She wants me inside and locked up before Dick gets here. She hasn't figured out that I could just unlock the door and leave. If I had someplace to go, that is.

"Honestly, Robin. You know I'm in a hurry."

"Okay!" All that's left of my Popsicle is a drippy sliver of purple ice. I work it with my tongue, licking it dry.

A horn sounds from around front. "That's Dick," Mother says. "Come inside now. There's a bowl of cut-up fruit in the refrigerator for your treat tonight." She goes in the house and I stand up.

I follow her indoors. "'Night, sweetie," she says, giving me a kiss on the head. "Don't stay up too late." She means she wants the living room cleared out so she can bring Dick home. I saw them having sex once on the couch. They were naked and smacked their bodies against each other again and again, making a bunch of noise. Then they collapsed in a heap. I only watched the one time, as it made me kind of nauseated.

I stare out the front window as Mother trots down the sidewalk to his car. He's a lawyer, divorced with two grown sons, except one of them is living with him, due to an emergency job loss.

I turn on the TV, thinking about my snack. Cut-up fruit. I've got a Nutsie Boy stashed in the back of the freezer, under a bag of frozen peas.

Two

I give a pale pink African violet a big gulp of water. It doesn't have much scent, but it still smells sweet somehow, living and green. It swallows the water right away, so I know it was thirsty. I can almost feel its relief. I've been taking my time watering everybody, talking to them and encouraging them to drink up. The Norfolk Island pine was depressed at first, but once I gave it a drink, pouring the water from its own special Mickey Mouse glass, it perked up. Plants are more emotional than you realize.

I pass the dollhouse on my way to the cacti and peek inside. The chaise lounge has been moved from the library to the master bedroom. The four-poster bed is now in the middle of the kitchen, the bedclothes disheveled. The kitchen table, with its red-checked tablecloth, is balanced on the roof, each dinner plate filled with a single M&M.

The cacti seem okay, so I move on to the rest of the African violets. I turned fifteen today, at 8:05 A.M., to be exact—two hours ago! My whole family is coming over for a cookout tonight—Dad and my stepmother, Janice, along with my older brother, Todd, and his wife, Serena. Melissa can't come, because her parents are making her go to a family party, all of the relatives getting together to say good-bye. It makes me mad that they're doing it tonight. They knew it was my birthday.

At least Frankie and China are coming. A couple of nights ago, China helped Mother pick out new curtains for our kitchen—she wants to be an interior decorator. She still seemed really happy to be with Frankie, so I guess it's good she doesn't know about the Ocean Side girls.

I give the last three African violets—two whites and a purple—a drink and carry the Norfolk Island pine's Mickey Mouse glass and the little plastic watering can to the kitchen. I wish Mrs. Jenkins would invest in an indoor watering hose—I'm sure I've seen them advertised somewhere—or at least buy a bigger watering can. It takes forever to—

I almost drop everything on the floor. Frankie's leaning against the kitchen counter in just a tiny pair of pale blue briefs, drinking a glass of orange juice and reading the comics.

It's not like I haven't seen him this undressed before—he walks around the backyard in his bikini all the time, and he's certainly not shy—but he's in his *underwear*. Isn't that kind of personal?

I'm surprised he's up this early. I know he bartended last night at Raze.

He glances up from the newspaper. "Hey, the birthday girl herself. Happy B-day, babe." He takes a sip of juice, studying me for a minute. "Fifteen. I remember fifteen."

He shakes his head and laughs, then goes back to his paper. The coffeepot starts to smell like coffee.

At fifteen he didn't have a big rear end. He'd just appeared in a print ad for Maxim's department store, modeling jeans. Girls were tripping all over themselves just to stand next to him. Mother looked at the ad in the *Chronicle* and said, "My." Just that. "My." I was only seven years old, but I remember that *my*.

I watch him read the paper now, smelling the toast right before it pops up in the toaster. He doesn't really have to watch what he eats yet, but Mother says he will soon enough. "That's the life of a model. And of an actor. Upkeep. Constant upkeep. That's true for everyone." She gives me this meaningful look. "Otherwise, the body just goes."

Frankie ignores his toast and keeps studying the paper. He's one of those people who read every single comic strip, even the stupid ones. I guess they're more pressing than melted butter on hot toast. By now I would have had it slathered and eaten.

Even though he has a tiny kitchen downstairs, he never eats there. I've seen the inside of his refrigerator. The only thing he keeps in it is bottled water, plus beer and wine. He says he never drinks before a job, because he can't afford to have a puffy face, but I know that isn't true. He drinks whenever he wants to, job or not. Puffiness just doesn't seem to stick to him.

I also know which drawer he keeps his drugs in. If you walk around to the back of the house, there's a small window at ground level. At night, with the lights on inside, you can see right into his bedroom.

He sets the comics aside and scratches his stomach,

flat and tan above his silky blue bikini briefs. Baby blue. He sees me looking at his drawers and laughs. "Harbingers, babe," he says. "The best brand there is." He gives me a wink. "If anybody asks, they feel *great*."

Not long ago he starred in this local commercial for Ted's Tires, playing a cute tire guy. This good-looking chick comes into the shop needing a new tire, and he gives the camera this big wink, saying, "Baby, I've got just what you need!" Everybody loved it.

Ever since this big success, he's been planning to move to L.A.

He picks up the paper again. "Me and China will drop by your cookout this evening, but just for a few minutes, okay? We've got this party to go to. Some guy with L.A. connections will be there."

He's met more guys with L.A. connections than you can count on ten toes, but his big career move still hasn't quite happened.

"Okay," I say to the newspaper in front of his face. Like *his* party is more important than mine? I let the door bang shut behind me.

"I'll be home later this afternoon," says Mother, heading for the door. Back from the bakery with my cake, she's now going shopping for other party stuff. "Enjoy the nursing home today. Let yourself meet some new people!"

Doesn't she realize that everyone in a nursing home is *old* people?

The door clicks shut behind her. I know she's not going shopping for a computer. She and Dad were supposed to get me one, but now she says it will have to wait till Christmas. She wants Todd to pick it out. It stinks when your only brother works with computers but is too busy to get one for *you.*

Mother is also shopping for a new dress. She's planning to keep Dick intrigued. She'll be gone all day.

My birthday cake box sits on the kitchen counter. I'm not supposed to see it till tonight, but as soon as her car pulls away I open the lid. It's perfect! Wide and flat, with *Happy Birthday Robin* written in dark blue, decorated with fat pink roses and green leaves. It smells like ripe sugar.

My mouth waters, so I shut the box. I don't have to leave for the nursing home yet—it's only six blocks away—so I head for Mother's exercise equipment. The one time I tried her rowing machine I almost pulled my arms out of their sockets, so I decide on the treadmill. If I exercise now I can eat more cake tonight, plus, if I keep it up, I won't look like a wrinkly sack of skin when I'm old. I turn it on and start walking.

"A woman has to keep up her appearance," Mother said, when she told me about spending a big chunk of my college money for the rowing machine and her facelift. She thinks tummies are the reason husbands leave wives—all those bellies blimped out by babies. That's what happened to *her*. She keeps herself in shape now, and has ever since I was six months old, when Dad left.

Still, she and Dad are both supposed to be saving for my education. Mother's an office manager for Metro Transit and doesn't exactly make a huge salary, so I don't know if my missing college fund will be replaced or not.

I keep walking. Not much is happening yet.

"Once you turn forty," Mother says, "men won't look

at you unless you're stunning. *Stunning.* And take my word for it—being all alone when you're older isn't any fun. I'm not going to end up like your grandmother."

Granddad left Nana for another woman on their twenty-sixth wedding anniversary, and Nana, who died when I was ten, spent the rest of her life sitting in a chair, looking out the window. *Silenced by tragedy,* Melissa says. Mother hasn't spoken to her father since he left. He's still alive somewhere, but I've never met him.

I'm breathing heavier now. This is working!

Ever since Mother got a facelift and a new boyfriend, she's been convinced that Mrs. Jenkins is jealous of her. Considering how good-looking Frankie is, Mrs. Jenkins is kind of plain, in a no-nonsense, businesslike way. In the early years of Frankie's career, when Mrs. Jenkins managed him, she ran *him* sort of like a business, deciding what jobs he should take, what clothes he should wear, what his image should be. Mother says it's a shame that Mrs. Jenkins pushed him like that, but it's not as though Mother doesn't enjoy the results.

Frankie's father left a long time ago and never even sent him a birthday card or a present or anything. "Like I care," says Frankie. "The guy's a shit. He'd better not try to contact me in L.A." He means when he's famous.

I speed up—maximum burn!

At least my dad visits with me and gives me presents and stuff. Janice, his third wife and second bimbo, is twenty-three years younger than Mother, twenty-five years younger than Dad. I think she's had a boob job, as her breasts look like they've been stuffed and mounted, but it's not something you can just ask. Especially since she doesn't like me very much.

I'm starting to sweat. I think my thighs might look a little trimmer.

Dad's previous spouse, Charlene, dumped him after only a year for some young guy in the Navy. Mother hasn't stopped laughing.

I'm panting. My thighs are definitely thinner!

When Mother and Dad broke up, they'd already been married a long time—my brother Todd is sixteen years older than me. "You were the final straw," Mother says, when she talks about her and Dad. I think about that piece of straw a lot.

I hop off the treadmill. My armpits are damp, my legs shaky. I flop on the floor and close my eyes, my heart pounding inside my chest. What's the point of exercise if you end up dying of a heart attack when you're only fifteen?

I try to block out the smell of the nursing home—pee and pine oil—by inhaling Mrs. Henley's lunch, but it pretty much stinks, too. Some kind of beef mush, with soft rice and canned green beans and a chocolate Dixie cup. I spoon up some beef and aim it at her mouth, managing to get most of it in. It's best not to watch too closely. She grins and gums while she eats, and the result is pretty nauseating.

If God had really meant for old people to live this long, he would have made them good-looking, with teeth, so teenagers trying to feed them wouldn't need to puke.

I close my eyes for one second and that's when I hear a little rustle. My eyes shoot open.

Mrs. Bothington! Before I can jump up, she's got Mrs. Henley's Dixie cup in her hand and is sprinting across the room like a greyhound. That's the second time this week! I start after her, out the door and down the hall, but she's gone. I stand with my hands on my hips. Why don't they enforce discipline around here? Do I look like a policeman?

I turn around and smack right into some guy, banging my nose against his arm. "Ow!"

"Sorry," he says, as I rub my nose. "You okay?" He's big, maybe a couple of years older than me, his skin the same color as his bushy mop of hair—light caramel, or maybe butterscotch. He's African American or something, mixed.

His left wrist is in a cast. He isn't wincing, so I must have hit the other arm.

"Is it swollen?" I ask, feeling my nose. "Today's my birthday. I don't want to look like Bozo the Clown."

He studies it seriously, and I start to blush. "Looks okay to me," he says. "No Bozo outbreak in sight." He steps back, as if to see me better, and tilts his head to the side, a smile playing over his lips. "No Bozo anywhere else, either."

My face goes up in flames.

His mouth opens in a silent laugh, his eyes crinkling up at the corners. "Well, then . . . happy birthday." He turns his head and his bushy mop of hair sways gently. "Um, do you know where 227 is? I'm looking for Miss Greely."

I point down the hall. "Room 227 is that way." I don't know who Miss Greely is.

"Thanks," he says, moving on.

I try not to watch him walk away.

* * *

Three o'clock. Birthday time! I sit on the front step. Melissa's supposed to come over to wish me a happy B-day before she has to leave for her family party. We met last September, at the beginning of school, when she plopped down in the seat next to mine in English, clutching a copy of *Romeo and Juliet* to her chest. "William, wherefore art thou?" she asked, her eyes shut tight. Then she looked at me, sighing deeply. "Don't you wish you could write like Shakespeare?"

I can barely write like *me*. Still, soon we were sitting together every day at lunch. She's leaving next week for Alabama. Her father, Mr. Crayber, got a new job there. I wish I'd met her sooner. A year of one person just isn't enough.

Alabama. I haven't heard of anybody else who's moved to Alabama. New York, New Jersey, yes. Connecticut, yes. California and Washington State, yes and yes. North Carolina. Plus Arizona. But not Alabama. I wish her parents hadn't decided to be such pioneers.

I pass the time by wiggling my toes. "This little piggy went to . . ."

On my fifth-grade farm day, when my entire class piled into buses and drove to the country, I saw a baby pig. It was beautiful. It looked like a pale, pink human baby, just in a piggy shape. The farmer picked it up to show us, and I wanted to hold it, stroke its little head, and give it kisses.

Todd and Serena have been trying for two years to have a baby. I've thought of telling them about the baby pig, how it looked so human, its little tiny eyes so sad, but I don't think they want a pig baby. They want a real one.

They'll be here for my cookout. So will Dad and the bimbo. And Dick. I wonder what kind of present Dick will give me. He doesn't know I've seen him naked.

I hear a whistle. Melissa! She zooms up the front walk. That's how she walks—she zooms. I have a hard time keeping up with her. She's everything I'm not: tall and skinny, with curly red hair. It sticks out all around her face like a mop. She's always trying to hold it down with barrettes or hair scrunchies, but nothing seems to work; in a few minutes it's loose and sticking out again. She's got a strong chin and a definite nose, with freckles that look like little tan ships sailing across an ocean of pale skin. I wish they weren't sailing away to Alabama.

She flops down beside me on the step, holding a plastic bag to the side. I know she's got my present.

"So how's fifteen?" she asks, giggling, her eyes darting between mine and the air in front of her face. She does that a lot, looking at the air when she talks. I don't know what she sees.

"Okay," I giggle back. Her birthday is next month.

She stretches her legs out in front of her. They're long and thin. Frankie says she came close to having a body suitable for modeling, but too bad about the face. Her face is fine! I honestly think that good-looking people don't always know what's good-looking. Melissa is the only girl I know who doesn't collapse when Frankie walks into a room. She calls him Mr. Studly. We got kicked out of English last spring for passing a note describing how to make Studlicious Frankie Pie. She came up with the part about topping him with whipped cream. That's the only time I ever got into trouble at school.

"So," I say. "What's in the bag?"

She laughs and aims her blue eyes at me. "Are we impatient, or what?" She makes me wait a minute, then swings the bag around and drops it in my lap.

I open it and pull out a thin box. White ribbon. Yellow paper decorated with white bunnies. Bunnies! How old does she think I am? I give her a look.

"It's left over from Max's party." He's her baby brother. She's got a couple more sprinkled in the middle. Max just turned one.

"Oh." He's the only baby I've ever held. He wiggled so much I almost dropped him, but fortunately, no one was looking. I pull off the ribbon and undo the paper. It's a flat, pale blue box. I open it. Paper. Beautiful thick sheets of pale, smoky blue paper, plus envelopes. I look at her.

Her eyes are dancing back and forth between mine and the air in front of her face. "So we can write," she says. "Real letters on real paper. Not just e-mail stuff." She rubs her nose. "Something beautiful, that we can keep." She smiles at the air.

Something beautiful. Suddenly my throat feels thick. Nobody ever said anything to me before about something beautiful, or about keeping it. I repeat it to myself. *Something beautiful.* I put the lid on the box. "Thank you," I say. My voice is wobbly. "I love it."

Frankie's front door slams shut. He's dressed completely in black. Tight black T-shirt, tight black jeans. He waves at us, adjusts his sunglasses, and gets into his car.

"So how's Mr. Studly doing these days?" asks Melissa, grinning.

"Studliciously!" I shriek.

We go inside and I get the big cake knife out of the drawer. I know I'm not supposed to touch it before tonight, but Melissa won't be here tonight. I cut two big pieces, topping each with a giant scoop of vanilla fudge ice cream.

Three

They're here! I open the front door before Todd and Serena can ring the bell.

"Hey, kid. Happy birthday." My brother gives me a half hug. It feels like being pressed against a two-by-four. He must have learned how to hug from trees.

"Happy birthday, honey!" Serena hands Mother my present, giving me this big, breasty embrace. Not because she's big or has big breasts. She doesn't. She just gets you in there somehow. She's as short and soft as Todd is tall and hard. I can't figure out how they ended up together.

Todd's already unhappy, ready to leave. "So, Dad here yet?" He's looking around the living room, as if our father might be hiding behind the couch. He can't forgive Dad his bimbos, number one or number two. Janice is only a year older than Todd.

"He's out back with Janice. And with Dick." Mother smiles in satisfaction. She's wearing snug blue jeans and a pale orange shirt that advertise her figure. I'm wearing tan shorts and a blue-checked blouse. There's nothing to advertise. What's the point of having a mother with big bazooms if you don't inherit them?

"Serena, be a dear and carry Robin's present out to the patio for me," Mother says. "I've got to get busy in the kitchen." She pats Todd on his face, but he jerks away. "Let me be your *mother,* Todd. Moms like to touch their kids once in a while." She rolls her eyes at Serena.

Always the peacemaker, Serena laughs, nudging Todd with her elbow, and follows Mother into the kitchen, which is how you get to the side door and around back to the patio. Todd and I watch her disappear.

During the week, Serena is a medical technician. On weekends she likes to get "untechnical" and go to flea markets and yard sales. I sometimes visit with her and Todd on the Saturdays I don't see Dad, and since Todd doesn't know what to do with me, I end up going with her. It's usually pretty fun.

"She's a nice girl and I'm glad Todd is happy," Mother said when they got married. "But she'll have to work to keep up her appearance." I think Mother's worried that Serena is future dumping material. She's got short, light brown hair and wears glasses. She isn't fat, but she's solidly built. Mother's holding her breath, hoping that she doesn't blimp out.

I guess Todd realizes he's alone with me, because he immediately starts toward the kitchen, too. "You coming?" he asks. I nod and join him. He left home for college when I was two years old, and, until he met Serena, returned only when he had to. I think the only time he really considers himself related to me is when we have to face the parents together.

* * *

I follow Todd across the patio and sit on one of the hard chairs we pulled out from the dining room. We have a cookout every year for my birthday, and we still don't have enough lawn chairs. I take a sip of Pepsi and belch, but it's the kind that nobody hears. Dick's doing the charcoal. He's got them squirted up, ready to fire. We're having barbecued chicken—my favorite—and potato salad. Plus a garden salad. Mother wants me to stick to the garden salad, but I think it's okay to eat potato salad on your birthday. I haven't lost any weight yet, but I still have the rest of the summer.

Dick's fairly tall and fit, with short gray hair and a trim gray beard. I guess he's okay to look at. Dad's kind of short, with salt-and-pepper hair, and his belly and rear end are a little bit round. Mother doesn't know how he keeps getting those bimbos.

Dick's trying to get a conversation going. It's almost working. He and Dad are talking business—Dad's a CPA with One Galaxy Bank; Dick's a lawyer, handling tax stuff.

Boring.

Todd sits in my favorite lawn chair, sipping the beer Dad handed him when we came out. They did the hearty handshake bit, then parted like they'd both touched a hot wire. *A tragic indifference,* Melissa says. Serena talks to the bimbo.

I guess it isn't really nice to keep calling her that. Janice is okay. She doesn't exactly like me, but it's not like she's stupid or a creep. She does public relations for Vita-brite, a vitamin health care line *For people who want to stay young.* That's their motto—it's written right on the label. Mother smirked when she heard it. "'*For people who want to stay young*? You mean there's someone who doesn't? Oh, please," she said. She also said Dad's the biggest fool in the world to think he can hold on to someone like Janice, but so far she hasn't bolted. Two months ago, he bought her a ring with five diamonds on it for their fifth anniversary.

Janice's hair is shoulder length, dark and shiny. She usually wears it down, but tonight it's pulled back in a ponytail. It *still* looks sexy. She's wearing tight white shorts, a blue halter top, and she's *tan*. This is not the kind of person you want for a stepmother.

My real mother comes out of the kitchen carrying a tray full of pretzels and potato chips and dip. Dick touches a match to the charcoal. Dad clears his throat, watching with alarm as the flame flares up from the grill. He leans forward, as if ready to douse it with his beer, should it be necessary. He's always on alert for disaster.

Frankie and China walk up.

Everybody's head turns. China, her honey-blond hair cascading to her shoulders, is wearing tight, low-cut Jaido jeans and a light yellow tank top that doesn't quite cover her navel. No bra. You can see her breasts moving under her shirt like they've got a private appointment with summer. You can see her nipples.

I close my eyes and try not to picture the girls of Ocean Side.

Now *her,* Mother said the first time she saw China—then didn't say anything. There was nothing to say.

Frankie's wearing the same kind of jeans, guy version, and a bluish green silky tee. He practically shimmers. He must have liked what he saw in the mirror today. He already looks like a movie star.

Nobody says anything. It's like all the words got sucked out of everybody's throat.

China's holding a silver designer shopping bag stuffed with purple tissue paper. She comes over, every eyeball following her, and reaches down to give me a hug. She smells like flowers. "Happy birthday, Robbie." She hands me the bag. "This is from me and Frankie."

Robbie. Nobody else calls me Robbie.

I look around, not sure what to do. My other presents are on a little table, waiting for the birthday-cake-and-ice-cream part of my party. Should I open this now?

Mother's eyes have attached themselves to Frankie. She drags them off to address China, saying, "China, dear, you must have something to drink." Then her eyes snap right back. Dick's eyes are glued to China's breasts, and so are Dad's—the grill forgotten. Todd stares at his beer.

I notice a quirky little eye movement between Frankie and Janice. Not exactly a movement. An eye dance. My throat goes dry. Then Janice looks down at her drink, smiling. Frankie's lips curve upward. I hear Dad cough.

"Hey, babe. Open it." Frankie's looking at me. China walks back to him and he puts his arm around her waist.

Mother nods, so I dig my hand down through the tissue paper, feeling something soft and silky. So it isn't wrapped, it's just in there. I pull it out.

"My," says Mother.

It's a nightgown. A flowing, shimmery, silky pink nightgown. My face gets hot. It isn't a *sexy* nightgown, not like the stuff Mother bought for her weekend away with Dick last month. Still, it's *sexy.* I've never had anything like it. It kind of scoops up under the breasts. It's just incredibly pretty. Soft and shiny, with little fancy stitches at the top. I don't know what to say.

"Like it?" asks Frankie. He looks up from nuzzling China's neck. "China picked it out."

I nod. Dad looks at it dubiously. Dick looks at China. Todd tries not to.

"It's lovely," says Mother. "Just lovely." She reaches and takes it from my hands, holding it up.

Serena doesn't say anything.

"Thank you," I say. China smiles at me, then laughs when Frankie munches her ear.

"Well, we've got to run, babe." Frankie fishes for his keys. "Got to connect with this L.A. dude." They wave good-bye and amble off. Everyone watches them go. It's like they take all the summer with them.

A little silence descends, then Janice gets up. "I think I'll go use the bathroom." She crosses the patio. Dad's eyes follow her like a guard dog's.

"That was nice of them," says Mother, taking a sip of beer. She hands me back the gown. "You'd better go put it away," she says. "You don't want to get barbecue sauce on it."

I get up and follow Janice inside, then go upstairs to my room. I want to try my nightgown on, but decide to wait till later, when everyone's gone. I lay it across my bed. It feels like a cloud.

When I go back downstairs, Dad's yelling at Janice in the kitchen, the quiet kind of yelling you do when you don't want anyone else to hear you. I stand outside the kitchen door at an angle. I can see them, but they can't see me unless they try. "So what was *that* all about?" His voice is furious.

"It was about exactly *nothing*!" She spits her words.

"I saw the way you looked at him!"

"Oh, like you weren't looking at his girlfriend?" Her face is hard.

"*Looking.* Looking to *look.* Not looking to make a date to fuck each other!"

Air gets stuck in my lungs.

"That's crazy!" Janice shouts. "*You're* crazy! I'm sick of you watching me every single second! I can't even *breathe* around you!" She turns on her heel and bangs out the side door, almost plowing into my mother.

For once Mother looks embarrassed. "Sorry," she says to Dad after a moment, stepping into the kitchen. "I was coming in to get the chicken."

Dad runs his hand through his hair. "If that little bastard so much as *touches* her—" He stops, sputtering for words.

"You mean Frankie?" She walks over to the refrigerator.

"I saw how they looked at each other!"

Mother smiles, opening the refrigerator door. "You're upset about nothing. Frankie looks at every beautiful woman that way." She reaches in.

"Yeah. Well." Dad watches Mother's rear end as she leans into the refrigerator. When she pulls out the platter of raw chicken and turns around, he looks away. "So what's he doing giving my daughter a night-gown?"

Mother sets the platter down on the counter. "It's not just from him. It's from China, too. They're in the *business,* Brad. Clothes, fashion—who knows, maybe even the movies someday. A nightgown means nothing.

Besides, he hardly has his eye on *Robin.* Honestly." She laughs and hands Dad two bottles of barbecue sauce.

"I don't like it." Dad grips the bottles.

Mother picks up the platter. "This is *Robin* we're talking about! And she's only just fifteen. True, a lot of girls at fifteen would be a problem. But Robin wouldn't know what to do with a boy, even if she had one to do something with." She heads for the side door. "Now go make up with your wife. We have a birthday party to get through."

Dad stands still a moment, then follows her. The door slams shut behind him.

I walk into the kitchen and stand at the counter. At the far end is my cake. I slide down and open the box. Mother had a fit when she saw the two missing pieces. But she doesn't know about the stationery Melissa gave me. She doesn't know about writing *something beautiful,* that we can keep.

I stick my finger in a blob of icing, then lick it off.

I picture my nightgown lying across my bed and can almost feel the silky material on my skin. Looking out the window over the sink, I see that Dad has slid his chair closer to Janice and is gripping her hand in his. She looks annoyed. He looks worried.

Dick pokes at the charcoal. Todd gets up for another beer. At the cooler he raises his eyebrows at Serena, who nods and gives him a smile. He smiles in response and pulls out two cans. When he gets back he hands her one, then tousles her hair. She laughs, reaches up, and grabs him by the neck. Pulling him close to whisper something, she gives him a kiss. When he sits down, he's laughing sheepishly. He doesn't look so stiff anymore, so much like a piece of wood.

Mother stands beside Dick and puts her hand on his shoulder. She's trying hard not to gloat.

When I try my nightgown on later, what will I look like? Little Robin fat butt? Or *something beautiful*?

Four

In the corner of Melissa's front yard is a maple tree. The branches droop so low that, in the summer, you can sit under them and the leaves make a kind of lacy, private green room. Private, that is, if Chet and Andrew, her two bratty middle brothers, stay away. Right now they're watching the moving guys finish loading up a huge truck with furniture and boxes.

I'm sitting on an old wooden bench under the tree, holding brother number three—Max. He's got curly red hair, just like Melissa. They're the only two—everyone else has brown. Maybe he'll end up as tall and skinny as she is, but right now he's short and fat. And strong—he just whacked me on the boob. It hurts, but I pretend it doesn't. What can you say to a one-year-old? Now he's laughing at one of those little white butterflies that look like flower petals until they move.

Melissa is sitting on the other end of the bench, holding a book on her knee, writing on a piece of tangerine-colored paper. She's got three barrettes doing hair duty, but they aren't helping much. Mother says she always looks like a mop in search of a dust bunny. I don't think that's a very nice thing to say. I think she looks *famous.*

I can't see what she's writing. The stationery is my birthday present to her, plus the pen she's writing with. It's one of those Lizard pens, with the long green tails. You can get different colors, with different-color inks, but I like the green one best. I had to give them to her early because she won't be here.

My throat gets tight when I think of that, so I rattle Max's rattle toy. He grabs it, giggling, and tries to eat it. Babies aren't too concerned about their diet. I know for a fact Max likes ice cream.

He probably won't even remember that he got born in Maryland.

I look through the maple leaves—you can see out better than you can see in. There's only a few more boxes to put in the truck. Chet and Andrew are still watching. They don't seem too upset that they're moving, except Melissa told me that Chet came into her room last night and woke her up, crying. I'm not supposed to let him know I know. He's twelve, and *sensitive.* Melissa thinks boys are sometimes worse than girls that way, but I'm not sure about that.

Mr. and Mrs. Crayber are busy packing up the station wagon. As soon as the truck leaves, they'll make a beeline for Mobile, Alabama. Mr. Crayber's new job starts Monday.

If I were a bee, I could follow.

Max starts squirming really hard. This is the part I don't care for much. Babies are like bars of soap. I'm hoping Melissa will notice and take him. It'd be terrible to drop him on his last day in Maryland.

She folds the piece of tangerine stationery in half and slips it into an envelope, then writes something on it. She sits back and grins, watching me wrestle with Max. "Trade ya," she says, laughing. She puts the envelope on the bench and reaches for Max. He presses his head against her chest, then gets all quiet and snuggly in her arms.

"Take it," Melissa says, nodding toward the envelope. She gives Max a kiss on top of his head and stares at the moving truck. "But don't read it till later."

My name is written in Lizard green ink. I hold the envelope in my hand. We both look out through the leaves, watching the moving guys load the last box. Melissa's dad talks with the movers; then they get into the truck and drive off. Everybody stands around looking at each other. A few neighbors have come over, and suddenly Melissa's mom is crying and hugging people, her dad is shaking hands, and Chet and Andrew are squabbling over who gets a window seat.

Melissa stands up, holding Max real close, so I can't see her face. We leave the maple bower and she hands him to her mother. Suddenly we clutch at each other, mashing ourselves together, tears running down our cheeks. I bury my face in her shoulder, holding on as long as I can, but then she's getting into the car and the neighbors are waving good-bye. Everybody watches the car pull out of the drive and move down the road, and then it's gone.

The neighbors drift away. I'm holding my letter from Melissa.

* * *

Nobody ever asks about what happens when something is over. They only want to know about the *something*. Like when there's an accident and an ambulance comes. Everybody listens and says "gosh" or "wow" or "was anybody hurt really bad?" But nobody ever asks what happens when the ambulance leaves and you're standing by yourself looking at an empty space on the road.

Nobody.

I'm listening to Flower Tanahill. Melissa's been gone a couple of hours, zooming south through Virginia. Mother's getting ready for her date with Dick. He gave me Flower's CD for my birthday, plus a pretty gold necklace with the letter R on it. He said he couldn't find one with my name written out. I like it a lot. Mother says it's quality.

As for the CD, I've never really listened to country before, but this is kind of nice. A couple of the songs make me want to cry. Why do people always get cheated on? I hope in real life Flower's boyfriend—whoever he is—isn't a cheat. She's real pretty, so I don't see why he should be. Except . . . well, I try not to think about Frankie and China. Mother hates country and she hates Flower. "Honestly," she says, *"Flower?"* But Dick likes country and he likes Flower, so Mother is working on her prejudices. She's got that wedding ring in mind.

I think Flower is a pretty name. At the nursing home yesterday, I called Mrs. Henley by her first name, thinking that might make her stop picking at her arm, over and over, and pay attention to the spoon of vanilla pudding I was holding to her lips. She looked at me in surprise, as if for a moment she remembered who she was. *Diana.*

It's dark out now. Melissa used to whistle a birdcall, then look at me and grin. It took me a while to figure out that she was imitating a robin.

Maybe they're most of the way through Virginia by now. They're going to drive till late, then take a motel room and start up all over again tomorrow and drive forever. I'm not sure how Mr. Crayber's going to make it to work by Monday morning. Max will soon be an Alabama baby. He probably won't even remember the night he left Maryland and drove through Virginia, the darkness coming down with a *whoosh.*

I haven't read my letter yet. I'm saving it for just before I go to bed. Maybe we'll all be sleeping at the same time—me and Melissa and Max, and Chet and Andrew, too. Maybe we'll even have the same dream.

Sweet tweet Robin, she writes, in Lizard green ink. I'm sitting on my bed, wearing my new nightgown, the one I got from Frankie and China. Looking down, I can see my breasts cupped in pink silk. The rest of me is a blob, but the nightgown helps hide it.

Into the Alabama sunburst south I go. Wherefore you, sweet tweet girl? Follow me to yummy tummy Maxabillion days of heat and sun and gulfy plains. Leafy rooms and windows loom. Follow! Follow!

Melissa always writes like she's a poet or something. I think I understand what she means.

Chew chew churn the miles between. What say you, tweetie girl? Zoomalicious distance closed, I see your face. Come along—cheep cheep trill! Follow?

Follow? I'm too young to drive. Mother would never let me take a bus or fly alone. I don't see how I'll ever see her again.

Remember me, Melissamess remembers you—forever always come come please?

Melissamess. She never called herself that before. I picture her hair, its crazy mess of red curls.

I put the letter down and walk over to the dresser. My box of Bad Girl makeup and the Forever gift bag are still in my underwear drawer. Rummaging around, I find Sassy Strawberry Lip Color and put it on. It makes me look like there's nothing on my face but a big red ugly mouth. I rub it off with a tissue.

I showed the makeup to Melissa once, and she quickly dusted my face with bright pink blush and painted on Wild Blue Yonder eyeshadow and Radiant Raspberry lipstick. I gave her a beauty mark and purple eyelids, then stroked Caramel Cutie on her mouth. "Studlicious!" she shrieked, looking at us both in the mirror. We collapsed backward on my bed, howling, then spent the next five minutes trying to stop laughing and sit up. Instead, we slid off the bed and landed on the floor with a thump.

What happens to a laugh when the sound is over? Is it still there? Is Melissamess laughing in my room even now?

I stand still and listen.

* * *

My flip-flops smack quietly across the yard. Frankie's car glows red on the side of his house from the streetlight. I heard him pull up an hour ago and heard two doors shut. So he brought China home with him.

My pink silky nightgown swirls around me as I walk. Are Melissa and her family in a motel room by now, asleep?

I feel like I'm wearing an evening gown. I've never been outside dressed like this before—it's like I'm taking my breasts for a walk. Is that what movie stars think when they wear a low-cut gown to the Academy Awards?

I walk around the back of Frankie's house. A light comes from his window, a small, low rectangle next to the ground. I stand beside it for a moment, then crouch down. I always worry that they'll see me, but so far they haven't.

Their skin is light and kind of glows, China's especially. Her naked breasts make me shivery and nervous. Frankie works them with his mouth, running his tongue over her skin like somebody spilled a milk shake all over her body.

And Frankie—well, he really is just about perfect. If he ever gets to L.A., he'll make a good movie star. His front part always scares me a little, but China isn't scared at all. She's like a welcoming committee for his privates.

They lift their faces away from each other and look at the TV. A video is running, of people having sex. I can see it, but only at an angle.

I watch a while longer, then stand up. I don't want to be outside when Mother gets home—I'd really be in trouble. I think they must have gone to Dick's place. Maybe his son had a date or something and isn't home.

I walk back across the lawn in the dark. I scrunch my shoulders together and let the straps of my nightgown slide off, stopping to tug it down to my waist. I hold it there, standing still a moment. My skin kind of glows, too, which surprises me. Maybe my breasts are even a little bit pretty. I start walking again. The air is warm and touches me all over, as if it likes me. Should I take my nightgown all the way off? But then I'd be naked, and what if somebody saw me? I'd get arrested. So I keep it on, just letting my breasts stay out. When I reach the edge of our patio, I stop.

The night air is kissing *me*—little Robin fat butt.

I pull my nightgown back up and go inside.

Five

I'm supposed to be spending Saturday with Dad, but instead I'm spending it with the bimbo. Dad had an emergency bank situation that he had to deal with right away, because he's leaving tonight for Cincinnati to attend the funeral of his boss's mother. The viewing is tomorrow, followed on Monday morning by the service and burial.

"Honestly," Mother said, when she heard he was going. "Talk about kissing up!" But I think it's nice to go to the funeral of someone you've never met. That way, if you bump into each other after you're dead, you'll already be acquainted.

I think Dad really had an emergency golf situation to deal with. Sunday morning is his usual playing time, so he'd miss it altogether this weekend if he didn't go today. Besides, he never knows what to do with me. So I'm helping Janice at her office, filing paperwork while she catches up on her Vita-brite stuff, working on her computer. She's not going to Cincinnati with Dad. She draws the line at funeral services.

She never knows what to do with me, either. I wouldn't mind a movie. A few months ago she took me to see *Hotz,* which was an R. I didn't tell Mother. But today Janice didn't say anything about a movie; she just drove straight to her office. I think she's in a bad mood.

I know she wants to start her own business—she's thinking of a cosmetics line—and with her experience and Dad's money skills, she probably has a decent shot. But just because it hasn't happened yet doesn't mean she should be grumpy with me *now.* Or make me file paperwork.

"'You're the trouble I like, girl, the trouble I need.'" She stops singing along with Ret and snaps off the radio. "That does it for today," she says, turning to me with a smile. I can see why guys like her. With her dark hair and pretty face and white teeth, she looks like a commercial for toothpaste. "Want to catch some lunch at Dodges?"

Dodges! No wonder she's in a better mood. It's a brand-new restaurant/club thing, right at the D.C. line. Frankie told me about it a couple of days ago. "It's *hot,*" he said, giving me this wink. I'd just finished picking dead leaves off his mother's African violets. I watched him have a happy mirror day, combing back his hair and moving his head this way and that, practicing his sexy tilt for the new commercial he's got lined up—he'll play a financial services guy. He doesn't have any lines, but he says his image is what will sell. When I left, the dollhouse stove was heating up a giant Frito on the front porch.

He'll probably meet new L.A. connections at Dodges.

Janice locks the Vita-brite office and I follow her to her car—a shiny black Toyota Celica. I climb in, wishing there was a way to do this without actually riding with her. As usual, she zooms in and out of traffic, blasting through yellow lights. My stomach clenches in a hard, painful knot. I pretend everything's okay, though.

It takes forever to find a place to park, but she finally stuffs the Celica into a tiny space three blocks away. We climb out. At least I'll be able to work off my lunch calories ahead of time. Walking down the street, though, I start to worry. The white T-shirt I'm wearing over my cutoffs has giant blue violets splashed on the front of it, so it gives you something to look at besides my rear end, but what if it isn't enough? Do they let fat people into Dodges?

"It's just lunch," Janice says, glancing at herself in the tall windows of the shops we pass. She's got on her movie-star sunglasses. "It doesn't matter what you're wearing." She fluffs out her hair in a jewelry store window. "Nothing ever happens till after dark, anyway." That's when Dodges morphs from a restaurant into a club. She leans down and looks at herself in the side mirror of a parked car, touching the corner of her mouth, smoothing her lipstick. "You look fine," she says, not looking at me. She's wearing tight black pants and a snug pink shirt with a scoop neck. As always, she's *dressed.*

When we actually get there, I'm a little disappointed. Janice is right—whatever happens at lunch doesn't matter. Mostly we're in a crowded restaurant that looks real short of L.A. connections. Our waiter, though, salivates over Janice like *she's* from L.A., so I guess she's happy.

"My hamburger's real good," I say, taking another bite. I've got their special ketchup sauce all over my fingers and french fries. A blob drops on my chin, and since my hamburger is already at mouth level, I use the bun to wipe it off. Janice doesn't notice. She's busy picking at her salad and looking around the restaurant. Maybe she ordered a salad so I would take the hint and get one, too, but I wanted a hamburger. Melissamess could eat a hundred Dodges hamburgers with special ketchup sauce and never get fat.

She's been gone a week.

I'm working on the last of my chocolate milk shake when Frankie walks in. What's he doing here? It's not *night.* "Frankie!" I yell, standing up and waving. My arm freezes midair as half the people in the restaurant turn to stare at me. I sit back down, my face burning. Janice, to my surprise, doesn't look disgusted with me. She smiles as Frankie comes up to our table.

"Hey, look who it is!" he says, laughing. "Little Robin red—" He stops, leaning down to kiss me on the forehead. My skin burns—I know the word he didn't use. And what's with this *kissing* business? I glare at him, and he pretends not to notice. He smells incredible, lightly sweet and spicy. I recognize the scent—Flute, for men. *She'll listen for your melody.* That's what it says in the ads. He held the bottle under my nose just yesterday. Now he's grinning at Janice. His smile is like a spotlight. Whoever he turns it on feels like a star. "Janice, nice to see you again. So how's it going in stepmother land?"

Stepmother land?

Janice dimples and laughs this little laugh. "Oh, please. Don't ask." She darts her eyes at me and blushes, then looks back at Frankie. "It's going perfectly *swell.* Robin and I are having a great lunch. So how are things with you?"

"Absolutely fine." His eyes are traveling from her face down to her chest. I bet by now every woman in the restaurant is looking at him, wishing his eyes would travel down *her* shirt. But Janice is the lucky one. "I'm meeting someone upstairs about a job," he says, his attention back on her face. Janice smiles and toys with her fork, pretending she doesn't have eyeball tracks all over her boobs.

"Oh," he continues, "I think I *am* interested in some of those products you were telling me about. I'd like to place an order."

When was she telling him about products?

He looks at me and smiles. "Need my vitamins," he explains. "Gotta stay healthy."

Janice pulls an order form out of her purse and hands it to him. "Call me at the office or on my cell phone. I'll take your order and arrange delivery."

He can't call her at home? I suck the last of my milk shake out of my glass as loudly as possible. She shoots me this look.

Frankie pockets the form. "Well, I'd better go. Catch you both later, okay?" He heads for the stairs, looking back over his shoulder at Janice as if he's leaving a trail of bread crumbs for her to follow.

Janice smiles to herself and pats her lips with her napkin. "That was a pleasant surprise," she says. "He's a good neighbor to you." She checks her face carefully in the mirror of her compact and applies fresh lipstick. "And I can always use another vitamin sale. Finished?" She looks directly at me, and I know I'm not supposed to say anything to Dad—he's jealous of every single man she talks to who isn't him. I give my milk shake a last loud suck and stand up.

Dodges can keep their stupid special ketchup sauce.

As soon as I climb out of Janice's Celica, I go inside and grab my box of smoky blue stationery and my purple Lizard pen and walk to Melissa's. I want to sit under the maple tree and start my first letter.

People are already moving into her house!

I can't believe it. I stand across the street and watch. A big U-Haul is backed up and parked in the driveway. Two black guys are lugging a chest of drawers in through the front door. A brown-skinned woman in jeans and a T-shirt stands next to the truck, shouting after them. "It goes down the hall, in the second bedroom!" She's got beaded hair, pulled back in a thick clump of a ponytail.

I watch as another African-American man and woman come around from the back of the van carrying a small orange recliner. The front door eats them. Then a young dark-skinned girl runs around from the side of the house, laughing and screeching—followed by another black kid, a boy. The woman tells them to get inside and they charge through the front door and disappear, the woman following them.

The house is now theirs. My stomach hurts, like someone punched it. I want my maple tree back.

There's an African-American family down the block on my street, plus one around the corner. Mother wasn't thrilled when they first moved in, several years ago, but now she just shrugs. The neighborhood is getting pretty speckled with different colors.

I like the different colors okay. But I don't like this.

Everything gets quiet for a few minutes. Nobody comes out of the house. I don't hear any voices. I only need a minute, just one, just enough to scoot under the tree and *be* there. Just enough to feel the last of Melissamess. What can happen? I walk quickly across the street, pause, then glide across the yard and step beneath the leaves.

My skin immediately turns a light, mottled green. It's like being underwater, under a green sea. Will Melissa go swimming in the Gulf? Maybe she'll be a mermaid, Max a little fat green merboy. Maybe—

"Hello? Who are you?"

I jerk my head toward the voice, astonished. Someone is sitting on the far end of the bench. Why didn't I see him? Maybe because he's green, too. His hair is a ragged, bushy shrub that kind of floats out from his head, but it isn't black. It's a light tan, the same color as the rest of him.

My jaw drops. It's the guy from the nursing home!

"Well, are you anybody at all?" His mouth opens in a laugh, except no sound comes out.

"You were at Collingsdale," I stammer. "Room 227. I ran into you."

He looks puzzled, then grins. "That's right. I was visiting Miss Greely. A neighbor."

"She's not there anymore," I blurt. I checked.

He studies me carefully with his underwater eyes. "She died."

"Oh. Sorry." My face burns. Did I think she went on vacation?

"How's your nose?"

I touch it automatically. "It's okay." I watch him continue to sit, splashed with green. "So what are you doing here?"

He raises his eyebrows. "Moving in. What does it look like?"

"Oh. I mean, right. So—where are you from?" It must be nearby. Melissamess is from Maryland, but now she's an Alabama girl.

"Over in Ridgeway. Not far."

"I know where that is."

He sees me looking at the cast on his lower left arm and wrist. "Wanna sign? Better hurry. I'm getting it off next week." Names are scrawled in black and blue and red and green.

I feel stupid, but I'm holding my purple Lizard pen so I step over, find an empty spot on his cast, and write *Robin.* I step back, then step forward again and add my last name. *Davis.*

He reads it and smiles. "Robin Davis. Bird-girl Davis." He tries to whistle, but it comes out flat and broken. He shrugs. "Never could do it right." He laughs that silent laugh again. "Can I borrow your pen?"

I nod and hand him my Lizard. He looks at it a minute, then lifts his eyebrows at me, twisting his mouth to the side. His greenish brown eyes crinkle up. "Can I borrow your arm?"

I giggle. This is silly. I reach my arm out. He leans forward and writes on my bare skin. It tickles. He finishes and leans back. I turn my arm to read it. *Tri Holland.* "Try?" I say. I know how to pronounce Holland.

"No . . . *Tri.* As in . . . maple tree. As in . . . oak tree.

Or . . . holly tree. Or . . . just plain *Tri*." His nose wrinkles in a laugh, as he pushes his raggedy hair back with his right hand.

"Tri." I've never heard a name like that before.

"Tri!" someone shouts. The front door is open now, and the woman with the beaded hair is looking in our direction. Can she see me?

Tri shrugs. "Gotta go." He stands up, holding his left arm. "I'm still good for unpacking boxes."

He parts the branches. "Bye, Robin," he says, and walks toward the house. The woman follows him inside.

I stare at my arm. *Tri*. As in . . . maple tree.

I go home and put on Flower, then open my box of stationery. Where's my purple Lizard pen?

Six

Mother can't stop laughing and looking at herself in the mirror. More to the point, she can't stop looking at the diamond on her left hand. So far she's tried on three different dresses, including the neon lime. The diamond glints just fine against all of them. She finally settles on the dark rose.

"You're going to have a *stepfather*!" she exclaims, grasping me by the arms. I can see tears in her eyes. She must really like him.

Dick proposed at lunch, while I was across town at Dodges with the bimbo, sucking back my chocolate milk shake. Tonight they're going out dancing to celebrate. She's already called about twenty people to tell them the good news.

She even yelled at Frankie half an hour ago when he pulled into the driveway, waving her arm and pointing at her left hand. He came over, held her hand up to the light, and smiled at her ring. "Nice!" he said. "Congratulations,

Claire." He kissed her on the cheek, then gave me a wink.

He still smelled like Flute. I wanted to ask him about his new job offer, but Mother pretty much had the conversation hogged. "Both you and China are invited to the wedding," she gushed. She didn't say anything about his mother.

"You bet," said Frankie. He tugged a hank of my hair and left. I didn't like being tugged.

Mother went back inside the house to make another phone call. I could still smell Frankie and Flute.

"Should I call your father?" Mother is teasing now, laughing outright. I know she wants to gloat. Dick makes more money than Dad, so maybe there's a bigger house in our future. Maybe I'll get my college money back. I remind her that Dad's on his way to Cincinnati. "Right," she says. "Your father is so *very* official. God forbid that anyone should die without him. Dick, thank goodness, likes to have *fun*!" She laughs again. If she could figure out an excuse to call the bimbo and brag, she would.

I hear a car pull up and Dick comes in. He kisses my mother on the lips, and I see that this is a different kind of kiss. An *I'm yours* kiss.

I've seen them naked. Will they look any different once they're married?

I'm not supposed to be outside at night—but what about my purple Lizard pen? I can't start my letter to Melissa without it. Mother and Dick are out celebrating their engagement, so nobody's home. I've got my flashlight. I don't really need it on the sidewalks, though, since the streetlights are on. I feel a little spooky being out in the neighborhood like this, but nobody attacks me or anything. I watch carefully but don't see any escaped Lizards.

I stand across the street from Melissa's house. The moving van is gone. Her yard is dark, the maple tree a big shadowy blob. Except—it's not her yard anymore. Light shows from the windows in the house, around the edges of curtains or shades or blinds. I remember when Serena and Todd moved into their house, how hard Serena and Mother worked to get the curtains up before dark. I guess they didn't want anybody looking in.

Which window is Tri's?

I cross the street and go into the yard real quietly, sneaking under the maple. The leaves rustle a bit when I push through the branches, but there's no wind or air moving. I pause a moment, then snap on the flashlight. Nobody comes running out of the house, so I shine it quickly over the bench. No Lizard. I look under the bench. No Lizard. I play it over the ground, over the stubby edges of tree roots sticking up and the few scraggly clumps of grass. Everything looks eerie and lonely. Not much grows under a maple tree. I run the light over the bench again. Where's my Lizard?

"Whatcha looking for?"

I stumble backward and land on my rump, crunching my spine all the way up to my neck. My dinner ends up somewhere in my esophagus. Tri squats down and takes the flashlight, shining it at me. I blink and he shifts the angle. I can see in the leftover light that his face is scrunched up, like he's puzzled. "There some kind of supernatural force here that keeps drawing you back?"

"My Lizard," I say. My voice comes out all breathless,

but that might be because my intestines are wrapped around my windpipe. "I'm looking for my Lizard."

"Lizard?" Tri looks confused; then a laugh bursts from his mouth. "Your *Lizard*!" He stands up, sticks the flashlight under his left arm above the cast, and offers me his free hand. I take it, as I can't see any other way to get up without looking like a total piggy.

He hands me back the flashlight. "It's inside. I found it on the bench earlier. Wait a minute." He disappears before I can say anything. I see light pour out the front door, then disappear. A minute later it floods out again and Tri shuts the door behind him. I hear him cross the yard; then he's under the tree handing me my Lizard.

"Ray was using it. Hope you don't mind." I look at him and he shrugs. "My little cousin. Leave anything lying around for five seconds and he thinks it's his."

I point the flashlight at my Lizard. It looks okay. I snap the light off. "What was he writing?"

Tri is pretty much just a large shape in the dark now. "Ray? Don't know. Kid stuff." I hear this little intake of air. "You live around here," he asks, "or are you just passing through?"

"I live on Wenter—about twenty minutes away. Walking, that is. My friend used to live here." I wait for a response, but don't get any. "Melissamess."

The front door lets out another flood of light. "Tri? Who's that you're talking to?" It's the woman with the pulled-back beaded hair, peering out into the yard.

Tri turns to face the house. "Someone whose friend used to live here," he calls out. "Melissamess!"

"Melissamess?" The woman shakes her head. "Tri, get your butt inside, would you?" She goes back into the house.

"Don't ever be a mean woman's nephew," he says, then turns to face me. "My car's out of commission. You need a twenty-minute walk home?"

Me? Nobody ever asked me if I needed a walk home before. I shake my head no, then realize he can't see me. "No," I say.

"Be careful, then, in case the oogie-boogies are out." He starts pushing his way through the branches.

Oogie-boogies? "What's an oogie-boogie?"

He stops, pulls back, and leans close. I can smell his breath. Peanuts, I think, plus vanilla ice cream and chocolate. Nutsie Boy breath? "Racists and robbers and rapists, oh my."

Racists and robbers and rapists? I can't move. There's a silence, then Tri takes my arm and pulls me out through the maple leaves. He takes the flashlight and flips it on in my face. "Sorry. I've scared the crap out of you." He turns off the flashlight. "I owe you one walk home. Hang on." He heads into the house, then a minute later comes back. "The mean aunt has given me a measly half hour, so we have to haul ass."

I follow him hurriedly across the lawn. "You live with your aunt?"

"Yeah. Plus my uncle and cousins. Come on."

We head down the street. His legs are longer than mine, so I'm speeding. It's like walking with Melissamess. At least I'm burning up a bunch of calories. We don't really say anything else, except when I give directions, which are pretty easy. He doesn't seem worried about finding his way home again. We slow down when I say, "Fourth house on the right," then stop altogether. I left the living room lights on, plus the porch light. Next door,

Frankie's Probe is parked in his driveway, so he's either home really early or going out really late. Maybe he's busy with China. Mrs. Jenkins is in Atlanta.

Tri crinkles his nose at my house. "The Robin's nest," he says. "Looks just like a Tri house." His eyes laugh at me.

I giggle, staring at him and his unkempt bush of sandy hair. It looks soft. I want to touch it with my fingers. He gives me a poke, his finger lingering on my arm for just one moment. "Better go in." He turns to leave.

"What about the oogie-boogies?" I ask. He's walking home alone.

He thumps his chest with his good arm. "Me big strong man," he booms. "Oogie-boogies no get *me*." He's all one color under the streetlight, like coffee with lots of milk in it. What if the racists get him? "Bye, Robin," he calls, then moves down the sidewalk.

"Bye." I watch him till the street bends. A car turns up my block and I step into a shadow—what if a neighbor sees me and tells Mother I was outside? It stops just beyond the streetlight next to Frankie's driveway and pulls into a big patch of black across the street from his house. I wait a minute, watching, then my lungs plug up. Janice glides like a snake toward Frankie's front door.

Her boobs *are* fake. China's change shape, depending on whether she's up or down or sideways, but Janice's look like balloons filled with helium and only change a little. That's just plain cheating. Frankie, though, acts like he's in a pie-eating contest.

They had their clothes off before they were even halfway across Frankie's bedroom. I could barely see what they were doing, it went so fast. Now they're sitting up facing each other, naked, smoking a joint. I've seen him smoke before, of course, alone and with China.

I never thought China would get cheated on *once*, much less twice.

I try not to think about my father.

Now they're going at it again, only slower. Frankie runs his mouth over her like a vacuum cleaner. His hands work her breasts like he's trying to play volleyball. He pushes her down on the bed and she arches her back.

My face starts to burn.

I pull back a moment, then press my ear to the window. I don't do this too often, as it puts my head right there and what if they see me? But neither Frankie nor China ever did, and Janice doesn't seem to be paying attention, either. I listen and hear a muffled, "Oh, Frankie!"

Oh, Frankie? I don't think that's too original. At least Mother came up with, "Do it, Dick! Do it!" which has a lot of *d*'s in it.

I look again. Frankie puts his face between her legs, and my skin ignites.

Nobody ever tells you if you're supposed to let your father know that his wife is having sex with your next-door neighbor.

I'm glad he's still in Cincinnati. At least the dead person will be nice to him.

* * *

Mrs. Jenkins has a huge, ancient pink geranium in the back room, the room that used to be Frankie's bedroom before he moved downstairs. His old bed, a twin, is still here, covered with a bedspread. The geranium sits right in the middle of this deeply set window, so there's lots of space for it. I worry about it, though, more than I worry about the other plants. Mrs. Jenkins never mentions it, so I'm pretty much on my own—sun, water, the whole bit. How much is too much? Should I give it some Miracle-Gro or something?

It fills up most of the window, but I can still see Frankie lying on a beach towel outside, soaking up rays. He's wearing a yellow bikini, which is not his best color. He's got a gig tomorrow, greeting people at a convention or something in Baltimore. He wasn't real clear about what it is, but he called it an acting job. Maybe it's a convention of plastic surgeons. Boobologists.

He sits up, then pulls himself to his feet, grabs the towel, and heads for the house. He doesn't need any plastic surgery. His privates bulge in his bikini—and I know they're not filled with helium. Janice knows it, too.

The geranium has its face pressed against the window, like it's trying to get out. It's got three big round heads of pale, rosy flowers, so I guess that's good. But it seems unhappy. If I turn it around, at least it'll be able to get some exercise by reaching back to the window again.

I grab the giant clay pot and start turning. It's really big. The stem and branch things are thick and gnarly, and it tries to hold on. I work harder, getting the whole pot in my arms. Leaves and flower petals fly everywhere, and a spicy scent fills my nose.

"Hey, babe. Whatcha doing?" Frankie lifts the pot

from my arms and sticks it back in the window so it's facing exactly the way it was before. He brushes a spot of potting soil off his arm, then picks a leaf off his chest. He sniffs it, smiling. "I love the way these things smell. Don't you?" He tickles me under the chin with it, then places it on my head.

Wearing just his bikini, he's practically naked. He's standing so close that I can smell him: geranium, plus summer—the way July smells just before a storm. If I moved my hand an inch or two, I could touch his privates.

His eyes penetrate mine for a moment with their blue intensity, and I get this funny feeling in my breasts, right at the tips. Something fluttery and buttery happens between my legs, and I have to squeeze them together to make it stop. Then his eyes flicker away. "Well, gotta get ready," he says. He steps back and plucks the leaf off my head, then hands it to me, smiling. "I'm meeting China."

He turns, looking back once just before he goes.

Seven

Dear Melissa—

I can't think of anything to say. Nothing interesting, that is.

Mother is engaged to Dick. Dad went to Cincinnati last weekend for a funeral. Not his own, though!

That sounds stupid. Why can't I write like Melissa? She's always reading poetry and stuff and gets A's in English. I chew the end of my purple Lizard pen, which is actually its tail. I had hoped to get a letter from *her* this week, but here it is Friday already, and nothing came. I guess it's really my turn to write, since she gave me a letter before she left. I don't have her phone number yet.

I thump my Lizard against the dining room table. Flower's on—"You stepped out, so I did too, now I'm the sorry girl." Should I write Flower a letter and tell her to keep an eye on her boyfriend? If China can get cheated on—*twice*—who's next?

At the nursing home today, I write, *Mr. Simmons pinched*

me on the fanny. I was scooting between his wheelchair and Mrs. Steadman's walker. I thought I had enough room.

When I glared at him, he grinned like a Cheshire cat. It was disgusting.

Mother's home from work early, setting up for her engagement party on the patio. It's mostly a beer-and-chicken-wing thing—she's ordered tubs of them from the Chicken Den, and Dick's taking care of the beer. A bunch of their coworkers are coming, plus some of the neighbors, including Mrs. Jenkins, who's in town for a change, and Frankie and China. Todd and Serena will be here. Todd's never liked any of Mother's boyfriends, but since they're getting married, maybe he'll start liking this one.

Bang! That's the kitchen door. "Robin! I need some help with the crepe paper!"

"Okay!" I yell back. "In a minute!" She wants it wrapped around the lawn chairs and picnic table and tiki torches. But what if the tiki torches set the crepe paper on fire? When I mentioned this earlier, she just rolled her eyes. "Please," she said. "Don't turn into your father on me." It's pathetic when mothers aren't concerned about fire safety. She even wants me to wrap crepe paper around the barbecue grill. We're not using it tonight, but still. When she isn't looking, I'll sneak a bucket of water under the forsythia bush.

I met the boy who moved into your house. His name is Tri. As in—maple tree. He's African American, but the color of light caramel. Wait, does that make him seem less African American or something? Melissa gets very charged about these things. I scratch out *but the color of light caramel* and draw double hatch marks over it. *He's very nice.*

I wish I knew how old he is. When you meet people in school, you can figure out more stuff about them. But just standing in the hallway of a nursing home, or under a maple tree, what can you know?

His hair is an untamed bush. No, that sounds bad. I scratch it out.

"Robin!"

"Okay! I'm coming!" I stick my letter in the stationery box and go outside.

There's a million people crowded on the patio. I try to squeeze my way between a fat man in shorts and a woman in a black halter top who keeps bumping against his arm, whooping these big shrieking laughs. He's laughing, too, his face red. I wish they'd quit whooping and let me through. Between cigarette smoke and beer, I'm trapped in Stinkville.

Frankie and China walk up. People get quiet and start moving aside, staring and making room, as if they're royalty. China's wearing some kind of short, lacy white dress. Parts of her show right through the tiny lace holes. Frankie's wearing a dark blue pullover and black pants.

"Mom couldn't make it," he says, giving Mother a kiss on the cheek and shaking Dick's hand. "Business."

"Everyone!" Mother shouts, giddy. "This is my good neighbor, Frankie Jenkins, and his girlfriend, China. Soon to be real-live movie stars!" She laughs and hugs them both, then hands each of them a beer. "They're almost as famous now as Dick and me!" She giggles and latches on to Dick, giving him a big kiss on the mouth. Everyone stops looking at China long enough to laugh and applaud, and Frankie takes a sip of his beer. He waves at me, then I see his face change and he looks away.

"Hi, sweetie." Dad puts his hand on my shoulder and my eyes bug. What's he doing here?

"Brad!" Mother shouts from across the patio. "So nice of you to drop by! Everyone, that's my very excellent ex-husband, Brad, and his lovely wife, Janice. Now, do we all get along, or what?" She laughs, waving her cup of beer in the air. "Help yourself to refreshments!"

Dad squeezes his way over to the keg, and I'm left standing with Janice. She's got on a short hot-pink spaghetti-strap dress with a low neck. Her breasts haven't deflated any from playing volleyball. Her hair is down on her shoulders, and her mouth is painted the same shade of pink as her dress. She *glistens.*

"So," Janice says. "How nice, that your mother's engaged." Her eyes, though, aren't looking at me as she talks. They're focused on Frankie. I watch Frankie's eyes dart around the crowd, as if they're looking for anyone except Janice to land on, but they end up on her anyway. His lips curve slowly into a private smile, and *her* lips turn into a toothpaste commercial. But then his mouth twitches to the side, as if he just remembered something unpleasant, and he looks down. When he looks up again his face is thoughtful.

I don't see him *thoughtful* too often. Depressed sometimes, yes. Who'd want to be in Maryland when you could be in L.A.?

He keeps his face serious for a moment, studying Janice. Then a slight smile touches his lips and he turns away. Reaching for China, he pulls her close and plants a big kiss on her mouth. You can almost hear a sigh from the patio, like everyone's sick with envy.

China surfaces for air and laughs. Janice's smile is gone.

"Want one?" Dad sticks a paper plate piled with chicken wings under Janice's nose, and she pulls back in disgust.

"Brad, please!" She stomps off, leaving Dad stuck with me. So he shoves the plate in my hands and follows her across the patio.

I cram a wing in my mouth and start ripping meat off the bone. Mother bought a big engagement cake, with *Congratulations Dick and Claire!* written on it, but she hasn't cut it yet. It's still in the kitchen. She'd kill me if I took a piece ahead of time. But no one cares about a dead chicken.

Dear Melissa, I write. I'm sitting up in bed, wearing the pink nightgown Frankie and China gave me. Maybe I shouldn't be wearing it, because of how Frankie cheated on China. And—well, I don't like to think about this part—because of how Dad got cheated on, too. Should I tell him?

The gown is so pretty that I don't really want to take it off. Is that wrong? It still cups my breasts as if they were beautiful, as if they were flowers—the way you might cup your hand around a peony. *Beautiful flowers,* I write.

Wait a minute! I can't say that. Melissa would think I'm nuts. Plus it doesn't make any sense. I scratch it out.

I thump my purple Lizard pen against the piece of stationery, then look at my breasts again. Does China have a nightgown this pretty? I've only seen her naked or in clothes.

Mother and Dick gave an engagement party tonight. It's over now—it's 1:30 in the morning! A whole bunch of people came, but I only knew some of them. Frankie and China dropped by.

Does she remember Mr. Studly? I wish her laugh was still here in the room with me.

Nothing burned down. No, I'd have to explain about the crepe paper and tiki torches, and maybe even the bucket of water. I scratch out *Nothing burned down* and stare at my bare feet.

I found one of your barrettes yesterday morning, under my dresser. It's the one with the tortoiseshell backing. It probably came flying off after a fight with some of her curls. *Do they have that kind in Alabama? If not, I can mail it.* Now her hair is Alabama hair.

Who ever thought writing a letter could be so hard? I lean forward, watching my breasts change shape. This kind of nightgown lets you see a lot. I lean back.

It's quiet out now. I wish I was sitting under your maple tree, holding Max. You could be writing me a letter again and you wouldn't have left yet.

What kind of house did Tri live in before he came here? If Melissa hadn't moved, where would he be living now? Maybe God slides us around like pieces on a chess-board. But why did He move Melissa all the way to Alabama? That isn't fair. Her family even goes to church.

Frankie's got his nose buried in the comics, but Mrs. Jenkins looks up from the table when I walk into their kitchen. I forgot she was home. Mother decided late last night, after lots of beer, that since Mrs. Jenkins is gone so much, she must have a man stashed away in another state. An *ugly* man.

Mrs. Jenkins smiles absentmindedly in my direction, then turns back to the paperwork spread out in front of her.

"Hey, babe," Frankie says, glancing up as he turns a page over. "Nice party last night." He and China didn't stay long.

He's in shorts and a T-shirt, drinking coffee, his plate pushed aside—I see leftover runny egg yolk and toast crust. He likes it when his mother's home to cook for him.

"Yes, I'm sorry I missed it," Mrs. Jenkins says, taking a sip of coffee. She punches the calculator in front of her and writes numbers on a sheet of paper. I don't know if she's working on her business stuff or Frankie's. She still helps him out a lot. "The plants look good."

Frankie laughs. "Read this one." He slides the comics in front of her and she smiles, adjusting it for her eyes. The rim of her coffee cup is imprinted with bright red smacks. Maybe there's an ugly man somewhere who's *right now* washing red lipstick off his face.

"Do you want me to do the plants today?" I ask.

She looks up from the paper and smiles vaguely. "That would be nice. Oh, your money's in the envelope on the counter."

She *is* good about paying me.

She looks at the comics page again and laughs. "Now, isn't *that* true," she says, sliding it back to Frankie. They lock eyes and chuckle together; then he continues reading.

Isn't *what* true? Frankie sees me glaring at him, so he hands me the paper, pointing out the comic. *Zits.* I've already read it. I pick up the watering can and head into the living room.

The dollhouse is in pristine shape, each tiny piece of furniture dusted and placed exactly where it's supposed to be—as if no one had ever touched it.

Frankie has one skinny little green plant in his basement apartment. It always looks sickly, but I keep watering it, thinking it might take heart. He doesn't know what kind of plant it is. "Something between living and dead," he says.

As I'm urging it to drink up, Frankie comes thumping down the steps, pulling off his T-shirt and tossing it onto a chair. I follow him into his bedroom.

"I think your plant's better," I say.

"Hmm?" He's already standing in front of the closet, whipping clothes back and forth on their hangers. He has more clothes than Melissamess has curls.

"The plant. It's better."

"I gotta get some new threads," he says, pulling a couple of shirts out and dumping them on the floor in disgust. He's always worried he won't be wearing the right thing. He stares at the pile, shoving his hands under the back of his shorts. Is he going to pull them off, too? But he just rests his hands on his rump.

"Watering plants is sort of like cooking, don't you think?"

"Huh?"

"Plants. They eat water and dirt and stuff. It's like I'm their cook. I think they can smell the water coming." I can see the top of Frankie's butt cheeks.

"I guess. Damn, look at the time. I gotta get cleaned up." He hooks his arm over his shoulder, trying to reach the center of his back. "Give me a scratch, would you, babe?"

I cross the space between us and scratch, going higher when he says higher, lower when he says lower. We have a little scratching ceremony until the itch is gone.

Eight

"At least I'm engaged. I'll be damned if I'm going to be a grandmother without having a husband!" Mother's standing at the kitchen counter, furiously peeling carrots. Skinny orange strips sail through the air.

"At least it'll come after my wedding. We can't have two big events at the same time." Mother chops the shaved carrots into chunks and drops them in a pot of water. Then she rests a while and takes a sip of beer. The beer lets me know that Serena's pregnancy is a big deal. Mother usually drinks only at parties and "events," as it shows on her face.

"Once you're fifty," she says, "you can't afford any facial disturbance."

She and Dick have set a wedding date: December 31, New Year's Eve. I think that's kind of nuts. What if you have a big fight on your anniversary? All those bottles of champagne would be lying around, just waiting to be whacked over somebody's head.

Serena and Todd have known about the baby for a while, but didn't say anything at the party last Friday. "We didn't want to elbow in on your happiness," Serena said, when they came over Sunday afternoon and told us. She probably really *didn't* want to elbow in—she's the kind of person who waits her turn. Maybe she doesn't know that Mother would simply have elbowed her right back out. Serena also doesn't know that Mother's afraid she'll turn into a blimp.

Todd spent the whole time they were here alternating between smiling at Serena and bending and smashing an empty Pepsi can into a flat wad of aluminum. I think he's happy, though. He didn't look like a piece of wood, and he didn't say "computer" once.

"I suppose I'll have to give her a shower. It would've been nice to have some time to just be a bride again, you know?" Mother takes another sip of beer, then shrugs. "Well, life goes on, doesn't it? I tell you one thing—this kid's gonna have a grandma who's hot!" She leans over and looks at her reflection in the microwave oven door, then picks up another carrot. "Once you have a niece or nephew, Robin, you'll have to set an example." She looks at me meaningfully. I'm pretty sure she's talking about incorrigible pigginess. "Dinner in twenty minutes," she adds.

I go into the living room and turn on the television. John Johnson, who hosts *Citizens' Round One,* asks a guest his opinion on the president's tax plan, then spends five minutes yelling at him for having such a stupid opinion. I never know what they're talking about, but I like to see John Johnson yell. Sometimes I turn off the sound and just watch his face. There's a lot you can learn about a person when you just look.

A letter from Melissa! I hold the tangerine envelope in my hand. My name and address are written in green ink. I let the lid of the mailbox slam shut. Real mail!

Frankie's front door opens and Mrs. Jenkins comes out. Frankie's right behind her, carrying her suitcase. He puts it into her trunk. She's off to Boston this time. I watch them kiss and hug good-bye. Frankie waves till she's down the street and turning the corner. He stands still a minute, then turns, sees me, and gives a limp wave. He looks unhappy, but he always does when she leaves. A *tragic unfulfillment,* Melissa used to say.

I flap my tangerine envelope in the air. "From Melissa!" I shout. Frankie half smiles and gives me a thumbs-up, then goes inside again. He's got a job starting tomorrow, a print ad for men's underwear. It's just a dorky brand, not Harbingers, and he might even end up in boxer shorts—but his rear end will still be somebody's highlight.

He's taking China to Dodges tonight for drinks and dinner. I asked him about facial disturbance, since he has a shoot tomorrow, but he just shrugged. I think he takes more beauty risks than usual when his mother leaves. I hope he doesn't decide to take more risks with Janice.

I go inside and flop on my bed.

Sweet tweet Robin, Melissa writes. *Hot humid tumid midnight madness wails. Tears bemoan, sad weeps beseech. Most down down south am I, a truly zillion Maxabillion miles away. Max Max says "Hi!" The bouncy boy begins to speak! School is soon hot hot too soon. Wherefore you?*

I never know what she's talking about, but somehow I do.

Write me write me tweeter girl. Melissamess needs

Robin speech. Cheep cheep hop hop, you whirlie bird, a Lizard-girl is darting darts!

One day in my backyard, shortly before she left, Melissa imitated a bird, the funny way they hop around on the ground. With her long stick legs, she looked like a flamingo, her arms flapping up and down and her red curls bouncing. I laughed so hard I almost made a fart. Then I saw Frankie staring at us from his backyard and my laugh tripped over my tongue and I choked. He was wearing tight jeans but no shirt, and though I've seen him dressed that way a hundred times before, he looked like a living commercial for Flute cologne.

But Melissa started hopping and flapping her arms even faster, finally turning and bending over, furiously wiggling her butt at him. He burst out laughing, shaking his head, then went inside. "Melissa's okay," he said later. He didn't even add, "Too bad about the face."

Has he ever thought that I'm okay?

Birdy-girl, Melissa waits. Write-write the magic Maryland words.

She's signed it *Immobile in Mobile,* and included her phone number.

Maybe Janice is a horny slut. Marty, the blond guy on the TV show *Bust!* says that all the time about Share, the blond girl with the really big breasts. Marty and Share, plus Pete, Frieda, and Cal, are good-looking cops at the beach. In this one episode, they're getting ready to go on a drug bust, when Share discovers she's left the top half of her bikini in their new sergeant's office. She stands with her arms crossed over her chest, so you can't see the sexy parts, but you can tell she's topless.

Marty and Share are the stupidest ones, but I don't see how any of them could really catch a criminal, even one with a bad sunburn. I've been watching the reruns. Mother wouldn't let me see it before, because they spend so much time enforcing the law while wearing bikinis, but now that she's busy being engaged, she's not paying as much attention. Maybe we'll even get cable.

Janice has every cable channel there is, even the sex ones. Maybe that's why she's a horny slut.

This morning we're walking up and down the aisles in Baby Boom. It's really crowded. I guess people go all out for babies on Saturdays. Janice is wearing pale yellow shorts and a pale yellow baby tee, so she fits right in with the color scheme. We're not here for Serena, though. Janice's friend Kelly is pregnant and someone's giving her a shower. We're here to make a purchase.

I keep peeking at Janice when she isn't looking, but post-Frankie she doesn't seem any different. I can't smell Flute on her, but I also can't smell Old Spice, which is what Dad uses.

I wanted to spend this morning writing a real letter to Melissa, one that isn't too stupid to mail, but it's my Saturday with Dad. Except it's turned out to be my Saturday with Janice. Dad had "business" to take care of this morning. It's supposed to rain tomorrow, so I think it was probably golf business. But sunshine and exercise are good for you, and Dad has to stay fit to keep up with the bimbo. He's already got that biscuit belly.

Janice and I are supposed to meet him for a late lunch, but I know it won't be at Dodges. Dad's idea of taking me out is to stop at Tootie's, along with a thousand other families, for a Goofy Grill and fries. We've been going there forever. He *still* asks me if I want the peanut butter grill, and he's *serious.* He doesn't even smile when he says it.

Janice studies the lineup of baby quilts. They're stacked on a huge shelf that covers an entire wall, reaching all the way to the ceiling. They come in big sets—quilt, blanket, and sheets bundled together in thick, clear plastic. Some have pictures of cows on them, some dogs, some butterflies. Et cetera, et cetera. It makes me kind of dizzy. How can you know ahead of time if a baby will like cows better than dogs?

When Mother saw Dick grin at the news of Serena's baby, she relaxed. Maybe she thought he'd get one whiff of spitup and bolt. Turns out, he's a baby man. What luck!

Janice, though, hasn't said a word about Serena's pregnancy. It'll be her stepgrandchild! Serena said Dad sounded mostly surprised at the news, as if he couldn't quite get the idea of "grandchild" wrapped around his head. I could tell she was hurt by this, but then she perked up, saying, "He's just not used to the idea of his son being a father!"

What if Dad and Janice have a baby?

"I think it's nice Serena's pregnant," I finally say. I'm wearing the new pair of jeans and the bright blue tank top that Janice and Dad gave me for my birthday, trying them out before school starts, but she hasn't even noticed. I'm nervous about the tank top, as it makes my breasts look like they're sticking out, plus it shows how the rest of me is a chunk. I'm keeping my arms folded tightly across my chest.

She shrugs. "Yes," she says. "I'm glad they're happy."

She doesn't sound glad. She's busy deciding between the cow and the dog. A little kid slams into me from the side and almost steps on my foot, so I go on toe alert. Why don't parents watch their children? I'm only wearing sandals.

She finally chooses the cow and calls an employee over to climb up the ladder and get a fresh one near the ceiling, as this one's been opened. Even though this guy isn't too hot-looking and has bad skin, he about trips and falls off the ladder because he keeps looking down at Janice.

When he dumps the package into the shopping cart—it takes up the whole basket—Janice rewards him by turning into a toothpaste commercial, flashing him this enormous smile. Maybe he thinks he's about to get a Frankie-night. Maybe he's forgotten he's got zits.

We leave Quilts and make our way to the checkout, where a million people are ahead of us. Janice picks a line. We slowly shuffle forward.

I see that fathers pushing loaded shopping carts and holding brand-new babies are staring at Janice, already being led astray. I put my head back down and fold my arms even more tightly across my chest.

Finally Janice slaps her cow package on the counter and we slide up toward the register. That's when I notice the price. Two hundred fifty dollars! That could be going toward my computer.

"Hey, Robin!"

"Tri!"

He grins at me as he works the cow package price ticket under the scanner. Pinned to the open flannel shirt he's wearing over a blue tee is an employee badge that says *Tri.* So now everybody knows his name. The cast on his left wrist has been replaced by a thick blue nylon brace.

Janice hands him her credit card and looks at me. "You know each other?" She isn't impressed.

"Evil spirits keep dragging her back to my house," he says. He laughs and punches buttons on the cash register. Then he looks at Janice, his face serious. "I suggest an exorcism."

Janice laughs and Tri's yellow-brown eyes light up. I study the counter. She's doing her sex thing on him, too.

I wish he'd hurry up and finish.

I wish he hadn't seen her.

"Let's go, honey." Janice picks up the package and starts toward the exit.

Honey? She's never called me *honey* before.

I catch Tri's eye. "Who's *that*?" he asks.

I shrug. "My stepmother."

His eyes widen and he laughs out loud. "Stepmother?" He shakes his head. "*Stepmother.* Whew." Then he leans over the counter and touches my arm. "Goose bumples," he says. I look down. I've got goose pimples from the cold. Arm zits.

He reaches with his pen and quickly connects enough bumps to make a crooked smiley face. I turn my arm to look at it, just as the guy behind me in line nudges me with his shopping cart. Can't he see I'm busy?

"Bye, Robin," Tri says softly, smiling. I realize I've let my arms open up, and my nipples are busy acting like horny sluts. I quickly cross my arms again and head toward the exit. Halfway there, I look back. Tri's waiting for the impatient customer to fish out his credit card. When he sees me, he grins and lifts his pen, then turns back to the customer.

If I was writing a letter to Melissa right now, I'd say *his face is a butterscotch dream.*

I get the peanut butter grill, even though it's for little kids. It's like a grilled cheese, only made with peanut butter. You can get it with jelly, too, but I like it plain. Janice and Dad are having the grilled ham, chewing as they discuss Janice's business plans. She's thinking that instead of starting a cosmetics line—*way* too expensive—she could open a shop that *sells* cosmetic lines. Dad's giving her advice. *Boring.*

Still, they seem relaxed or something, maybe even happy. I guess her Frankie-night is still a secret, and Dad doesn't know about her being a horny slut. Maybe there's a parallel universe for liars. In that universe, Janice and Frankie are naked and smoking pot, playing volleyball with her breasts. In *this* universe, Janice and Dad are eating ham sandwiches and discussing face powder, while Frankie and China are together somewhere being gorgeous, busy becoming movie stars.

I pull the crust off my peanut butter grill. I like to save it for last. Dad is the only one I haven't seen naked yet. Maybe in *this* universe I won't have to.

Nine

On the way back from Tootie's, I ask Dad to drop me off at the Quick Mart, so I can get my Nutsie Boy stash for tonight. Except I don't tell him that. I say I need some Maalox. This works, since I kind of stunk up the car. For some reason, the peanut butter grill gave me really bad gas. It did that the last time, too.

When I get in the house, holding the Nutsie Boy bag behind my back so she can't see it, I find Mother sitting on the couch, crying. I almost drop my Nutsie Boy. "It's over," she sobs, mascara streaking from her eyes. "Dick and me. It's all over!"

"Why?"

"He doesn't love me," she wails, wiping her face with a tissue. "He's already cheating!" More tears spill from her eyes. "Well, I told *him*! I'm not the fool he thinks I am. I can find another man like *that*!" She snaps her fingers, then bursts out crying again.

Dick *cheated*? For some reason, I didn't expect that—maybe because he likes babies. I feel slightly dizzy.

Mother reaches for another tissue, her eyes red and puffy. All this crying probably isn't helping her face stay lifted.

I feel a big burble in my gut—more gas from the peanut butter grill. I try to make it to the kitchen before another eruption, but a stinky explodes, and Mother stops crying long enough to exclaim, "Oh, honestly, Robin!" I scoot out of the room, put my Nutsie Boy in the freezer, then go upstairs to the bathroom. It's not like adults never break wind.

When I come down later, pretty much degassed, Frankie is sitting beside Mother on the couch, his arm across her shoulders. "Claire, it's no big deal," he says. He's wearing a turquoise bikini and sandals, his chest bare—Mother must have dragged him in from sunning. "Guys look at skin mags all the time." He gives me a wink across the room.

"That's all very well for *you* to say," she sobs. "China *looks* like a Bunny! I look like, like—"

"Like a beautiful woman with mascara running down her face," he says, giving her a kiss on the forehead. "Now go call Dick and make up."

She sniffs loudly, then gets up to go use the phone in her bedroom.

Frankie looks at me and laughs, stretching his arms over his head. "Poor guy. She caught him with a *Playboy*." He rolls his eyes, then stands up. "*Playboy*. Your mom's just a little bit crazy, you know? Sweet and all, but crazy. You'd think she'd be past that by now, but hey—*women*."

He tousles my hair as he walks by. Even after the door

shuts behind him, I let my hair stay tousled.

I can still feel his fingertips on my head.

Mother's facelift has survived. By the time Dick shows up with a big bunch of red roses, she acts all sheepish and teary, making a big fuss out of putting them in a vase. When she and Dick disappear into her room, I play Flower really loud, so I won't have to hear her say, "Do it, Dick! Do it!" A while later they come out, laughing and happy like it's Christmas morning. It kind of makes me sick. On the couch late at night is one thing, but in her bedroom during the day?

Dick decides to make macaroni salad and grill hamburgers for dinner. He's got a knack for cooking, Mother says. A *knack*.

They usually go out on Saturday night, but they decide to spend the entire evening at home. I guess they need to recover from the nuclear Bunny attack, but with them here, I'm out of Nutsie Boy luck. All I get for dessert is a cup of fruit cocktail. We watch an old *Star Trek*, followed by *Reality Cops*, then *Desperate's Way*.

I hate *Desperate's Way*. Thomasina is this mother who has cancer, which she has to fight each episode while at the same time buoying up her family's flagging spirits. Some weeks she's doing well, some weeks she's not. Some weeks it's chemo, some weeks it's radiation. Some weeks Bif and Tallie, her teenage son and daughter, are starting to have sex with all the wrong people. Some weeks Ed, her husband—because of all the stress and everything—*wants* to have sex with all the wrong people, even though he really loves Thomasina. So far he's remained faithful, but you never know. *Every* week the show's pretty nauseating.

On my own, I always hit the remote once I figure out what kind of week it is, but Mother wants to watch it. I hand her *TV Guide* so she can just read the blurb instead, but she ignores me, sniffling through the whole thing while Dick squeezes her hand sympathetically. It kind of disgusts me that he does that, but I guess it's good he's squeezing her hand instead of somebody else's boob.

I think *Desperate's Way* would be better if they just went ahead and killed off Thomasina and let Bif and Tallie and Ed have sex with all the wrong people. The ratings would go up.

When the show's finally over, I ask if I can watch *Bust!* but Mother won't let me.

At one-thirty in the morning, you'd think the sky would be ink, but it has a pale, icky cast to it, I guess from all the streetlights. How is anyone supposed to navigate by stars anymore? There aren't any. What if somebody had to find his way north by the Underground Railroad or something, reading the stars for directions? He wouldn't make it. He'd have to camp out at the Doughnut Glaze till daybreak.

I don't see any lights on in Tri's house, but you never know when someone's going to get up to use the bathroom, then decide to go for a walk. That's what happened to me. I cross the yard and sit on the bench under the maple tree. Bugs are chirping and hissing like crazy, but so far nothing has bitten me. Insects weren't on my mind when I left home.

I quietly tear open the paper wrapped around my

Nutsie Boy. I don't exactly need the flashlight to see what I'm doing, but it *is* a little spooky sitting in the dark. The streetlight across the road helps a bit, gleaming through the leaves and branches. I didn't get attacked by the oogie-boogies on my way over, but what if a poisonous bug, a giant spider or something, smells my Nutsie Boy and decides to bite me?

I chomp into chocolate and peanuts, getting a good hunk of vanilla ice cream. It's pretty soft by now. I had to sneak into the kitchen and open the freezer door real quietly, hoping Mother wouldn't wake up and hear bags of lima beans and corn being pushed aside.

Actually, I had to hope that neither Mother nor Dick woke up. He hasn't slept over before, as Mother doesn't believe in doing that when there's a kid around, but I guess now that they're engaged, I'll have to watch him scramble eggs and fry bacon every Sunday morning. Dinner is one thing, but *breakfast*? What if I forget to put on my robe and he sees me in my nightgown? What if he forgets to put on his pants and I see him in his underwear?

Nutsie Boys are always done before you want them to be. I lick my fingers clean, then feel for the stationery box on the bench beside me. My purple Lizard pen is rolling around inside. I flick on the flashlight and wait a minute. Nobody comes running out of the house.

Dear Melissa, I write. It's kind of hard to do this in the dark, balancing the box on my knee and holding the flashlight at the same time. *Mother and Dick had a big fight today, over Playboy Bunnies.* No, that sounds stupid. Plus she might think they're perverts or something. I scratch it out and thump my pen against the page. *At night, the bugs sound bigger.* Well, they do. *I'm visiting the maple tree in front of your old house. Does your new house have a maple tree in the yard?* Maybe they don't even have maple trees in Alabama; maybe they just have special southern trees. *I think it's interesting that Tri's name sounds just like "tree." I mean, since there's a maple tree right here.* No, that sounds like I'm a moron.

I wish Melissamess was sitting here beside me right now and I didn't have to write her a letter at all. We could just talk. I never thought to sneak over at night when she lived here. A good idea too late.

A car comes slowly up the road, so I flick off the flashlight, my heart speeding up. The darkness is even worse than before—I can't see *anything.*

The car stops—right in front of the house! In the movies, it's best to be prepared, so I stand up. Quietly, I sneak over to peer out through the branches, ready to run. Why didn't I at least bring a steak knife with me?

The driver opens the door. *Tri!* What's he doing out so late?

I hold my breath as he starts across the yard, his shoes crunching the grass. They stop crunching. When they start up again—it's in my direction! I start clawing my way out through the branches at the same time he pushes his way in. When he grabs me, my voice is a strangled squeak in my throat, and I almost pee my pants.

He stares at me through the darkness, pushing a branch away from my face. Then I hear a quiet laugh. "Racists and robbers and rapists, oh my!"

I burst into tears.

* * *

"Easy, Robin," he says, his voice low and tense. "I'm sorry I scared you, really. But could you please dry it up?" My face is pressed into my hands as he awkwardly pats my shoulder. "I seriously don't want to wake up my aunt." We're sitting on the bench, just close enough to barely touch.

"I'm *crying*," I blurt, snuffling into my palms. "I can't just *dry it up*." I wipe my eyes and cheeks, then dig a tissue out of my pocket. "Maybe your aunt should wear earplugs to bed." I don't care if his entire household is awake.

"Earplugs. There's an idea." Tri sighs and leans back against the tree. "I saw the reflectors on your sneaks," he says, keeping his voice low, "in the light from the street lamp." Sniffling, I can just see his face, all shadowy and dark. "So you're still channeling Melissa?"

"No! I'm writing—"

He puts his finger on my lips. *"Please?"*

I whisper. "I'm writing her a letter."

"No kidding?" he whispers back. "This is exactly where *I* come when I want to write a letter. The bench under the maple tree, at two o'clock in the morning! Have we got something in common, or what? Wanna go steady?"

My face gets hot, even though I know it's just a joke. "Well, why are *you* here?" I'm pretty sure Baby Boom isn't open all night. All the customers would be at home, making babies.

"I'm here because I live here!" he whispers loudly. He shifts on the bench and his arm brushes mine, resting there. "I was visiting my mom. I was planning to stay the night, but . . ." The heat from his skin tingles. Should I move my arm back? Body parts are complicated. He half turns to face me, and I lose his arm. "Your parental types know you're out?"

"Not exactly."

"Better go home, then. I'll give you a ride. We need to be quiet, though." He stands up, starting to move from under the tree, so I do, too. "The mean aunt will throw me in the dungeon for sure if she nabs me with a girl in hand—especially a girl like you."

"Like *me*?" I duck and put my hands up as a branch tries to smack me in the face. "What's so wrong with *me*?"

"Uh." He entwines the misbehaving branch with another so it will stay put. "How's about, um, *nothing*?" We stand still a minute, staring each other down, then he smiles and touches my arm, and we're crossing the lawn. We climb into his car—a lump of gray metal—and glide away. But when we turn the corner at the end of his block, he pulls over and stops, looking at me. "How old are you, Robin?"

"Fifteen."

He laughs. "Good. I was starting to think you might be an overdeveloped twelve-year-old who's just really bad at running away from home."

Overdeveloped twelve-year-old? "So how old are you?" My voice comes out all snarly.

"Hey—no biting, okay?" His eyes glint in the light from a street lamp. "I just turned seventeen. Actually, I'm thinking of running away from home myself, but not till Thanksgiving. You know, after we cut the pumpkin pie." He turns his head away, his voice trailing through the darkness like the smoke when you blow out a match.

"I like pumpkin pie."

He turns, a grin touching his mouth as he surveys my shape. "No shit."

I fold my lips tight.

"Hey, that's not an insult. I like a pie-eating woman."

"Really?" I'm so shocked, I realize too late that I've spoken out loud.

"Sure. When it comes to dessert, pie *rules.* Anybody with any sense knows that."

I open my mouth, but before I can say anything, he continues. "And now for the other pesky little question. What color are you, Robin bird?"

"Color? White. I guess." I look at my arm in the dark. Maybe I could work on a tan.

"Hmm. Just as I suspected. You see, the mean aunt has very exact color standards for her surrogate offspring." He rubs his nose with the back of his hand. "She can't forgive my mom for producing such a bleached-out kid like me for her to raise. So I have to bring the color standards back up. The mean aunt gets nervous whenever I share my Gummi Bears with a white chick."

"Oh."

"So we can't go steady after all."

I start to giggle and he laughs, starting up the engine again. I glance at him while he's driving, then look at my lap. Nobody ever tells you what to say when you get a ride home with a butterscotch boy.

The sky is still pasty, with no stars. "You know," I say, politely, "if African Americans like yourself had to use the Underground Railroad today, you wouldn't be able to, because all the stars are washed out from the electric lights and everything, and no one could rely on them for directions. There would have to be a new travel plan."

This is something the mean aunt might not have thought of. She might even be grateful for the information, once she wakes up.

Tri is silent a moment. "Well," he finally says, clearing his throat, "good point. I guess everybody would just have to join AAA and get one of those TripTik things and drive." He smiles at me. "Glad to know you're thinking of us, Robin." He doesn't say anything more.

When we pull up in front of my house, we sit for a minute. No lights are on, so Mother hasn't discovered I'm missing.

"Give me your stationery box." I hand it to him and watch him open it, pick up my Lizard pen, pull out a clean piece of paper, and write something on it, leaning toward the light from the street lamp. "The next time you need to channel evil spirits at two o'clock in the morning, say this spell three times before you leave the house." He hands the sheet to me and I tilt it toward the streetlight. *Underground, Overground, Sis Boom Bah. Oogie-boogies, Mean Aunts, Ha Ha Ha.*

I look up to find him watching my face. "Works for me," he says.

In the dim light from the street lamp, his face is pale, full of sandy light and dark shadows. He relaxes into a smile, and I see how soft his lips are.

I slip the piece of paper into the box and hold it against my chest. "Have you ever had *chocolate* pie?"

He snorts so loudly, I look at my house to see if anyone's snapping on lights. "Go on," he says, laughing, nudging me. "I'll wait till you're inside."

I slide out of the car, shut the door quietly, and walk up the sidewalk, wishing I was still sitting next to him. I unlock the front door, waving as he starts to pull away, and step inside. As soon as he's gone, I step back out. The night air is damp and warm; I want to say good night to it. School starts next week. Why didn't I ask Tri where he'll be going?

I can still feel the warmth of his arm, where it brushed against mine. Maybe I should go put on my nightgown, the pink one China and—

I catch a movement out of the corner of my eye. Turning, I see Frankie leaning against the side of his car, arms folded, watching me.

Ten

Ten

"Robin! Phone! It's Melissa!"

I trip on the tie of my robe and almost kill myself stampeding down the steps, retying it as I run so Dick won't see me in my nightgown. It would serve Mother right, though, if I fell and broke my neck. Why won't she let me have my own phone?

I fly past Dick, who's standing in the living room reading a piece of the Sunday paper. He smiles at me and waves a spatula as I tear past him into the kitchen. Mother's leaning against the counter in her silky black robe, laughing into the receiver, sipping a cup of coffee.

"Oh," she says. "Here she is. Nice talking to you, hon." She hands me the phone and waltzes out the door to join Dick and his spatula. Fortunately, everyone is wearing some kind of clothing.

"Melissa!"

"Robin!"

We're silent a moment, then we both start giggling at the same time.

"Why haven't you written?" she finally asks.

"I've *tried*. And *tried*! But everything I say comes out goofy." Are her curls still fighting with each other? Are they still punching out barrettes? "I found one of your hair clips."

"Which one?"

"A tortoiseshell. Under my dresser. I can mail it to you." Why didn't I do that before?

"Wow. I got my hair cut really short a week ago. I don't even use barrettes now."

"Really?" She cut her curls off?

"It's really hot and humid here. What's it like in Maryland?"

"Oh. Well," I say, giggling, "it's hot and humid."

"Yeah, but down here, it's *really* hot and humid. It's like living in a sauna."

"Oh." I've never been in a sauna. "So how's Max?" Has he turned into a merboy, swimming in the greeny gulf?

"Fat! Fat and bad! Fat bad Max!" She laughs. "Right now he's eating the phone cord. You get a computer yet?"

"No."

"Darn. We could at least do e-mail." I hear someone in the background. "Okay," she says, voice muffled. Then she's talking in my ear again. "*Write* me. A real letter. Send me some bodacious words!"

Bo—what? "Um, okay. I—"

"Gotta go. Mom's worried about the phone bill—as if *she* isn't the one who's always yakking long-distance! Plus I'm meeting this girl. She's showing me around and stuff."

"Girl?"

"Grace. She lives a couple streets over from me."

"Oh."

Melissa's quiet for a moment. "I miss you, tweeter girl."

"Me too. I mean, you."

"*Write* me, okay?"

"Okay."

We say good-bye and I hang up. A package of bacon and a carton of eggs are sitting out on the counter. All that stands between cooking and eating is me. I leave the kitchen so Dick can get going.

Upstairs, I sit on my bed, then reach for my stationery box on the nightstand and pull out a sheet of pale, smoky blue paper and my purple Lizard pen.

Dear Melissa, I start—then cross it out.

Dear Nobody in Particular, I write. *Melissa has a new friend. Her name is Grace.*

One of Mrs. Jenkins's maidenhair ferns looks pale and sickly. What if it dies while she's away? You'd think someone with so many plants wouldn't take a job where she has to travel so much.

I hear a noise behind me and turn. Frankie's finally out of bed, unshaven, holding a mug of coffee, wearing a loosely tied terry-cloth robe. It looks brand-new, white and puffy.

"So who's your boyfriend?" he asks, taking a sip and staring at me over the rim of the mug. His hair isn't combed yet. A little puffiness shows around his eyes—so he isn't puff-proof after all. I bet he hasn't even brushed his teeth yet. Still, it's disgusting how good-looking people are good-looking even when they're temporarily unattractive.

"Boyfriend?" I was hoping he'd forgotten about seeing me last night.

He sets his mug down next to the ailing fern. Will the coffee fumes bother it? It doesn't seem to notice, but with plants you never know.

"Duh! The guy who brought you home *wa-a-y* after dark." He plays with the tie on his robe while staring at me, and I can't help but wonder—is he naked underneath?

"Oh." I give the African violet a little sip of water. What would happen if I gave all the plants a cup of coffee? That might perk them right up.

Frankie reaches out and takes my arm, turning me toward him. I notice that the tie on his robe has come undone, but the robe is still together and I can't see anything. "He's not my boyfriend," I say, still holding the plastic watering can.

Frankie scratches his chest, opening the robe just a little. He's wearing some kind of underwear. Probably Harbingers. Definitely white. The robe closes up again when he stops scratching. "Look, babe, two o'clock in the morning, plus boy, plus girl, equals *something.*"

I shrug. "He just gave me a ride home, that's all. From Melissa's." Frankie knows perfectly good and well that piggies don't have boyfriends. Although Tri does like girls who eat pie.

"I thought Melissa moved to Louisiana or something."

"Alabama." I've told him a thousand times. "He lives where she used to."

Frankie shrugs and his robe opens again, this time all

the way, and it stays open. *Thong* Harbingers. "Okay, whatever." Then he lifts my chin and looks me right in the eyes. "But before you get to the hot and sweaty stuff, talk to me first, okay, babe? We don't want any accidents."

Accidents? Hot and sweaty stuff? My face starts to burn. Frankie leans down and places a sour, coffee-smelling kiss on my mouth, dead center. Then he picks up his mug, takes a sip, and walks toward the kitchen.

My face shoots up in flames. I dip a little water out of the plastic watering can and rub it over my skin, trying to cool it. When I finally go into the kitchen for a refill, Frankie's downstairs, Ret blaring from his sound system. He and Janice like the same kind of music.

I wore the bright blue tank top Dad and Janice gave me for my birthday, but nobody's noticing. Everyone's looking at Shayna and Teresa. Everybody was looking at them last year, too. Just two girls can suck up all the boys.

Tenth grade. I guess Tri's a senior. I haven't seen him, but I keep looking. Maybe he goes to another school.

I *hate* eating in the cafeteria. But if I go outside, I'll be all alone. Here—okay, I'm still all alone, but that's what happens in cafeterias. Everybody knows that you have to eat *somewhere.* Outside, though, everybody has at least one friend.

I don't think I'll find a new friend this year. Nobody could replace Melissa.

At least in the cafeteria, you can buy stuff, like Twinkies. Mother packed an apple for me with my sandwich, but who wants to eat an apple at school? When they see the apple, everybody knows you're fat and on a diet.

I break one of my Twinkies apart, lengthwise, and lick out the creme filling. I study the result—a Twinkie boat! Then I eat it up and do the other half. I've still got a whole Twinkie left to look forward to before my next class, which is Spanish. In the meantime, I rummage in my backpack for the book I'm reading, *Annabelle's Secret.* Annabelle is sixteen and pregnant, and her boyfriend wants them to run away to Montana together and live on a ranch. She has to decide if she wants to raise horses and babies at the same time, or have an abortion.

Instead of *Annabelle's Secret,* though, my hand accidentally grabs my stationery box, so I pull it out.

Dear Nobody in Particular, I write. *Last year I had a friend to sit with outside. Melissa.*

"Hey! Robin! Wanna ride?"

I whip my head around. *Tri.* He's half in and half out of his car, waving at me. A ride! Kids are getting into cars right and left.

"Come on! I've got to get to work."

He must mean Baby Boom. I hurry over. In the daylight his car looks like I thought it would—an old, gray dump, a used Ford Escort. Janice would never be caught dead in it.

There's a faint sheen to his face, probably because it's so hot out. He's still the color of light caramel—skin, hair, eyes, everything—like a light brown sugar you're not supposed to eat. He's wearing a dark blue Tay-man T-shirt and baggy jeans. "So how was your first day back?"

"Okay." I climb in. "I didn't know if you went here."

He settles behind the wheel and grins. "Only when

I'm not away at Prep."

"Your hair's shorter." Just a little. It's still a tangly, floppy bush.

He starts the car and laughs. "Only when I can't escape the mean aunt."

It just takes a few minutes to get to my house. I wish it took longer. I stare at the front door. I wish I lived somewhere else and he would drive me there.

I start to undo the seat belt and discover that the shoulder strap is making my left breast stick out—as if holding it up on display for everyone to see. I practically rip the belt off. "Thanks for the ride," I mumble.

"No problem," Tri says, watching as I start to exit. "By the way," he adds, smiling. "Nice shirt."

I bang my head against the top of the door frame.

He takes off and I walk to my door, rubbing my head. *Nice shirt.* I look down at my bright blue breasts. Nobody ever said that to me before.

With the start of school, my time volunteering at the nursing home is over. But yesterday I went to the demento ward to say good-bye to Mrs. Henley. *Diana,* I yelled, right in her ear. She blinked and grinned, her eyes coming into some kind of pale, fuzzy blue focus. Then she drooled on her chin and fell asleep.

Bye.

The first batch of gingersnaps comes out charred, with black bottoms. I use the spatula to slide them off the cookie sheet and into the trash can. I'd forgotten how important timing can be. Serena's still lying down in the living room on the couch, so maybe she won't notice that part of the recipe is missing.

Todd is painting the baby's room this weekend, so she came over last night to stay with me and Mother. Everything, including paint fumes, is making her puke these days. Mother left the house early this morning to shop for her wedding dress. I think it's too soon to start shopping, as there's still plenty of time for her and Dick to break up.

I grab the last gingersnap before it lands in the trash and take a bite. It tastes burnt, plus it's hot and I burn my tongue. I *hate* it when that happens. I stick my tongue under the faucet and run cold water over it, getting my face and T-shirt all wet. I blot off with a paper towel, then get another lump of dough ready to shape into balls. Serena showed me how to do it.

Her tummy doesn't really look much bigger yet, but it wasn't exactly flat to begin with. When the baby comes out, will it look like her or Todd? Mother says Todd looked like a ghost when he was born—long and pale and silky.

"What did *I* look like?" I asked her this morning, as she was getting dressed to go wedding-dress shopping. Serena was still in bed, upstairs in Todd's old room.

Sitting at her vanity table, Mother studied herself critically in the mirror. "Bobbin," she said.

"Bob—what?"

"*Bobbin.* Like on a sewing machine." She carefully applied Chocolate Cherry lipstick to her lips, then blotted her mouth with a tissue and fluffed up her hair. "There," she said. "I think I look damned good for a grandmother-to-be." She had on her short magenta shirtdress.

"Bobbin? Like on a sewing machine?"

She slipped on her heels and tucked a fresh tissue in her purse, then paused. "No, more like in that old song about the red robin. You know—the one who comes bobbin' along." She laughed, chucking me under the chin. "Honestly, Robin, you're so *serious* about everything—just like your father! Try to relax once in a while, would you? I'm *joking*. You were my sweet baby girl, round and fat, with fuzzy brown hair." She opened her purse again and rummaged. "Now, where did I leave my car keys? That's right, on the hutch." I followed her into the living room. "I've got to run to beat the crowds. Don't pester Serena to death today, okay, honey?" She tore out the door.

I looked like a round, fat piece of sewing machine? No wonder Dad left.

The second batch of gingersnaps comes out okay. Flower's singing, and I think it helps. Even cookies probably like musical accompaniment. I'm just putting in the third batch when "Sorry Girl" starts. Uh-oh. I hope cookies don't get depressed.

"Smells great, honey!" Serena gives me a hug, then sits on one of the kitchen stools and runs her fingers through her hair. Last night after she went to bed, Mother commented that Serena's hair looked like a Grade Four hurricane. It still does.

"What smells so good?"

We both look up. China! What's she doing here? She laughs nervously. "Nobody heard me knock. The front door was open, so—well, hope you don't mind." Her hair doesn't look like a hurricane. It looks like she just got ready for a gig at the Playboy Mansion.

"Come on in," says Serena. "Robin's baking cookies. Help yourself."

China smiles and crosses the kitchen floor. She's just wearing jeans and a black tee, but she still looks like a movie star.

"Congratulations on the baby!" China gives Serena a hug and Serena hugs back, laughing. But when they part, China's eyes have tears in them. She looks at me, trying to keep her face from crumbling. "Your mom home?"

I'm still holding the spatula. "Uh, no. She's out shopping for her wedding dress."

China laughs over her tears, tossing back her mane of hair. "Wedding dress! Of course! I tell you, a wedding, a baby—you folks are sure keeping busy over here."

Her face is red and her eyes are turning an amazing dark color, like the bottom of the ocean or something.

"China, what's wrong?" Serena's already good at being a mother.

China bursts into tears. "Frankie! I think he's cheating on me!"

"Oh, no!" Serena gathers China in her arms while I stand as stiff as the spatula.

The cookies turn suicidal and burn.

Eleven

When Mother walks in from shopping, her lipstick is all worn off and her hair is mashed flat. "What a day!" she exclaims, tossing her keys on the hutch.

I turn down the volume on *Terminator 2.* I've already seen it about a billion times.

"I think I tried on every dress at the mall. Not *one* of them—well, there was *one* possibility, a short cream with a great little boxy jacket—but the others! Hopeless. Next week—why, China! What a pleasant surprise."

China and Serena are coming in from the kitchen.

"You're just the person I need! Someone who knows *clothes.* You've *got* to come with me next time!" She drops her purse on the couch and runs her fingers through her hair. "With your expertise—honey, what's wrong?"

I guess she just noticed that China's hair now looks like a Grade 4 hurricane. Plus her eyes are red, and in a Christmas emergency, Rudolph could make good use of her nose.

I turn the volume back up as the good Terminator guy tries to kill the bad Terminator guy all over again. What I don't need to watch is *Cheating 2*.

Dear Melissa, I write. *China thinks Frankie's messing around behind her back, but she doesn't have any evidence. Just a "feeling."*

When your father's wife's boyfriend's girlfriend has a *feeling* she's being cheated on, should you say something? It's not *my* fault that Frankie played volleyball with Janice.

I scratch out what I've written, wad it into a ball, and toss it into the wastebasket. I never had any feeling at all that Melissa would find a new friend, especially one named Grace.

Mother thinks China's feeling about being cheated on is wrong, especially since there's no evidence. "Frankie adores you!" she told her. "Have faith!"

She almost broke up with Dick over a nuclear Bunny attack, but now she's acting like Thomasina on *Desperate's Way*. "Have faith!" is exactly what Thomasina says at some point every week, even though everybody's busy trying to have sex with all the wrong people. "You're imagining things," Mother said, giving China a big hug. "Frankie likes all beautiful women. But he loves *you*!"

She has never even heard of the parallel universe.

The mean aunt looks at me like I'm a horny slut. I'm at the Quick Mart, two Nutsie Boy cones bagged behind my back. She and Tri are also at the Quick Mart. We ran into each other, except it feels more like the mean aunt ran over me, then backed up to take another hit.

Tri's holding a bag of ice, grimacing, I guess, from the cold. I feel a chill, too, creeping up my wrists from my hands, even though I'm wearing my long-sleeved pink T-shirt.

"Aunt Betsy, this is Robin."

"Davis," I add, for some reason. Aunt *Betsy*? I thought it would be something like Laetitia.

"Robin Davis," Tri repeats. "She's the mad channeler I told you about."

"Hmm." The mean aunt's eyes are dark brown and shiny. Her face is medium brown and wide, her lips painted a deep red. Her hair is still pulled back and tied into a thick ponytail, but it's braided now in a bunch of skinny braids instead of beaded. She's not fat or anything, but she also isn't exactly thin. Mother would definitely put her on blimp alert.

She hates me.

"Hello, Robin."

"Hello, um—?"

Tri jumps in. "Mrs. Beech."

Beach? Betsy Beach? "Hello, Mrs. Beach."

She glances at Tri, then reaches to take the ice. "Grab a bag of charcoal and meet me at the register." She turns to me. "Nice to meet you, Robin," she says, her eyes flickering over me like dark, evil wishes. Then she heads up front. "Ray! Becky! Come on!"

Tri mentioned a Ray, but Becky? Becky and Betsy Beach? Didn't the mean aunt and her husband think things through carefully before they got married?

A black kid, maybe eight or nine, with close-cropped

hair, starts to tear past, then stops and grins. "Hi!" he says.

Tri rolls his eyes. "Beat it, Ray-gun."

Ray shrugs. "It's my birthday," he says to me, laughing. "Cookout! Barbecued chicken!" He kind of wiggles around, like he's got fleas, then charges after his mother.

"Cookout?" That's what I had. "Isn't it kind of chilly for a cookout?" Why is this kid using *my* birthday idea?

"We barbecue anything, anytime," says Tri. "Sun, snow, rain, dead of night—doesn't matter." He laughs. "Chicken, hot dogs, snakes, stinky little cousins—if we can stick it on a grill, we cook it."

A girl, maybe a year or so older than Ray, clomps up behind Tri and leans against him, peering around his arm. When she sees me, she starts to giggle. "So who's your *gir-r-r-l*friend, Tri?" Her hair's knotted into little fat black bumpy things all over her head.

Tri shakes her off. "She's not my *gir-r-r-l*friend, Becky. She's a world-famous channeler of evil spirits."

She looks up at Tri, her dark face intent and filled with doubt. "Really? Naw!" She laughs and stares at me. "Really?"

"Sure," I say, shrugging. "Ghosts, spirits, bugaboos."

"She's the best," adds Tri. "Nationwide." Becky's eyes narrow in suspicion.

"Tri! Becky! I'm leaving!" The mean aunt's voice booms through the entire store. True, the Quick Mart is pretty small, but still. Tri raises his eyebrows and laughs. "Come on, Beck-womp, before we're disowned by your ma and locked in the shed without our supper."

Becky giggles and dances a little up-and-down dip thing. "No barbecued chicken!" she cries.

"No cake!" Tri shouts.

"No ice cream!"

"No sodas! Not one!"

"No chips! No dips!"

Their voices get louder with each word, and my face gets hotter. A few other people in the store turn to look. Should I pretend I'm not here? Plus they're basically describing *my* birthday.

The mean aunt steps around a rack of potato chips, eyebrows lifted. "You two about finished?"

Tri bends forward from the waist, sweeping his right arm downward in a bow. "Your wish is not our command, Aunt Betsiness. Nonetheless, we obey."

Her mouth twitches, like she's trying to hide a smile. "Obey, my foot. Now where's Ray at?" She nods at me briefly, then disappears behind the potato-chip rack. "Ray! Up front!"

Tri grins, and I forget about being embarrassed.

"Bye, Robin."

"Bye, Robin," Becky mimics, her voice high and squeaky.

Tri frowns. "Beat it, Beck-womp." He gives her a light smack on the rear end and she charges toward the front of the store. "Ma! Tri *hit* me!"

Tri's face flushes and he scrunches his eyes shut. Then he opens them, half laughing. "Never be a bratty girl's cousin," he says, shrugging. His eyes meet mine, then glance away. I've never seen him embarrassed before.

I don't know what to say. Of course I'm not his girlfriend. My fingers are numb and my arms are about frozen up to my shoulders by now from the Nutsie Boys I'm holding behind my back. I'm about to drop them, so I have no choice but to swing my arms forward.

"Private party?" Tri asks, taking in the evidence.

I shrug, my face growing hot.

He lifts my chin with his finger, which surprises me, and studies me intently. "Just as I suspected," he says. "Energy depletion brought on by too much late-night channeling. Remedy: two Nutsie Boys. Plus general avoidance of ghosts, bugaboos, and spirits."

"Tri! Charcoal!"

His finger disappears from under my chin. "Bye, then." He turns to leave. "Oh," he says, looking back. "Nice shirt."

I haven't seen Tri in a couple of weeks, though I wore my long-sleeved pink tee to school twice. I mean, I've seen him here and there, like at the other end of a hall, but we haven't talked or anything. He waves when he sees me, so that's something—but he hasn't offered me any more rides home. Maybe he's upset that someone mistook me for his girlfriend.

I'm spending Saturday with Serena and Todd, except I'm really spending it with Serena, helping her clean, since she's pregnant and all. Todd's working on his computer. He did call me Aunt Robin when I walked in, and even smiled. I hadn't thought of myself as officially *Aunt* Robin before. I've never been anything except *Robin.*

Under the couch is a dust bunny the size of Texas, plus—uh-oh—a *Penthouse.* I pull it out, shake the dust off, then march into Todd's study. *Somebody* around here has to start thinking about the baby.

Todd turns the color of cherry pie filling when I ask him—*meaningfully*—what he wants me to do with it. He snatches it out of my hand, mumbles something about taking care of it, then sticks it under a pile of papers. He turns to his computer again, dismissing me, but I can see that the backs of his ears are bright red.

I return to the couch, aim the mop, and begin to extract the dust monster.

"Todd told me you found the *Penthouse*!" Serena blurts out, right behind me. I bang my wrist really hard against the underside of the couch. "You should've seen his face!"

I rub my arm. You'd think she'd be embarrassed, but she can't stop laughing. This baby will definitely need me.

Mother fixes me a beef patty and a green salad for dinner. She and Dick are going out.

When she leaves the kitchen to start her bath, I butter a couple of slices of bread and slap on some ketchup—now the patty doesn't taste so bad. I check my Nutsie Boy stash, then head over to Frankie's to tend the plants, since Mrs. Jenkins is away in Albany again. Plants are such individualists. *They* decide when and if they want water.

Frankie's red Probe is in the driveway, but when I get inside the house, I don't see or hear him. Maybe he's asleep downstairs or something, or maybe China picked him up.

In the living room, the tiny lights in the dollhouse are on, casting a weird glow over the furniture. The chest of drawers in the master bedroom is tipped over, the dining room hutch is lying flat on its nose, and bitsy dishes are scattered across the rug.

•

A bad mirror day.

I finish watering—the Norfolk Island pine drinks *two* Mickey Mouse glasses of water!—then listen at the top of the basement steps. I don't hear anything, so I start down to Frankie's apartment. In truth, his little plant may be dying, but that's all the more reason to pay attention to it. I pour in a dollop of water. "Swallow," I say, in encouragement. You want the last word a plant hears to be a friendly one.

Bang! What's that? I drop the watering can, spinning to run back upstairs. Instead, I step on something hard and round, slipping off it, stumbling sideways. I fall against Frankie, grabbing him to keep from landing on the floor.

"Sorry," he mumbles, holding on to me, slurring his words. "Dropped it."

Shocked, I pull myself upright, pushing away, heat roaring through my body. He stinks of alcohol, his hair a mess, his face unshaven, his eyes bloodshot. It's more than that, though—he's *naked.*

Shaking, I make myself look at the empty wine bottle on the floor. Frankie bends to pick it up, almost losing his balance. I grab his arm, pulling him upright; he sways but doesn't fall over. He's drunk, I guess. Stoned, too, maybe. I don't know what all he is. His eyes can't seem to focus right. At different times I've seen him smoke pot or drink booze or swallow pills, but he's never looked or acted like *this.*

I try to pretend that everything is normal.

I've seen him naked before, of course, when I've watched through the window, but I've never actually been in the room with him. I can't help looking at his privates.

His *thing* is there, hanging out from a nest of dark, silky hair. I could touch it.

He kind of belches out some garbled words, then puts his hand on the top of my head and just stands there. His face is all puffy and blotched, and when I try to move from under his hand he starts crying.

He pulls me close, hugging and weeping, mumbling words I can't understand. I stand still—we're like two clothespins trying to dance—but he walks me backward into his bedroom. We land on the bed.

My body goes rigid, but his keeps moving. He runs his face, slobbery and stinky with alcohol, all over mine. His tongue lands in my mouth, and his hands fumble, trying to get under my sweatshirt, under my sweatpants, between my legs.

I struggle to push him off—we're having this weird, slow wrestling match—but he's still on top of me, still crying, still saying words I can't understand. Panicked, I *shove,* and he rolls away without resistance, lying still on his back. I scramble off the bed and run to the door—and he calls out. What did he say? I pause, my heart banging in my chest. He cries out again, tears on his face—and I realize he doesn't even know it's me. I swallow hard, my heartbeat slowing down. This is *Frankie.* He's just had one too many pills. He's quiet now, his face wet, his eyes shut. He looks cold.

I go back to the bed, pulling at his blankets to cover him. When I reach across his chest, he grabs my hand and holds it, then drags it down to his *thing.* Stunned, I pull back, but—

"Please," he mumbles, as if he's begging me. "Please." I feel myself let it happen, as if I was watching this from a distance, maybe in a slow-motion movie.

I touch his *penis.*

It's floppy and soft, kind of wrinkly. Under my hand, though, under both our hands, it begins to get bigger, then hard and incredibly smooth. He groans, and I feel a weird excitement—*I'm* doing this, not China or Janice. Suddenly he shudders violently, his body twitching and jerking, his eyes rolling back in his head. Then he collapses, his limbs falling motionless, limp.

He's not breathing. I've killed him!

Mother's just buttoning up her long-sleeved blue sweater-dress when I run screaming into her room. She charges over to Frankie's, me at her heels. He *is* breathing! But though she shakes him and calls his name, he won't wake up. She dials 911.

She pulls a blanket around him and cradles him in her arms until the emergency people arrive. My voice all breathy and scratchy, I explain about watering his plant, about finding him. I don't mention the part about touching.

Dick pulls up just as Frankie is loaded into the ambulance, so he drives Mother and me to the hospital. Soon China comes running in and she and Mother clutch each other and weep. I feel dark and slimy.

It turns out he's okay, though. Too many drugs and too much booze. The doctor doesn't say anything about him being touched. They pump him out, and except for temporary facial disturbance, he's fine. China takes him home.

* * *

It's really late when we get back from the hospital, but Dick makes hot chocolate, stirring the milk and cocoa and sugar in a saucepan as Mother paces the floor and exclaims repeatedly, "That boy! He's like a son to me! How could this happen? How? It's all those fast people he hangs out with. They'll give you whatever drug you want—cocaine, that ecstasy stuff, speed, whatever—just like that." She snaps her fingers. "Thank God China knows to stay away from it. Those drugs are poison!"

I've seen China smoke pot with Frankie, but decide to keep quiet. Maybe there's a lot of things I shouldn't talk about.

Dick puts extra marshmallows in my cup and smiles and touches me briefly on the head when he hands it to me. I smile back, weakly. How did he know I like extra marshmallows? I don't even deserve *one.* The cup is heavy in my hand. The next time China touches Frankie, will she sense *me*?

Mother barely tastes her cocoa. When she walks Dick to the door to say good night, I finish her chocolate for her. I'm practically a criminal anyway.

Mother goes into her bedroom to call Mrs. Jenkins again—she's been trying all night. She must finally reach her, because I hear her talking, voice muffled.

I open *People* magazine. Lucinda Lave, the latest Bond girl, has a new boyfriend, Ricky Dan, who recently broke up with his wife, Connie Britton, in the middle of filming *Two Man Tango.* They'd been married only eighteen months, so I guess it wasn't that big of a deal. A friend says she's never seen Lucinda look happier. Connie's mending her broken heart by dating baseball slugger Wayne Gem.

Everybody cheats in Hollywood, so maybe touching someone else's boyfriend's *thing* is not unusual.

You can tell that Lucinda's boobs are bigger than Connie's, so that might have had something to do with Connie and Ricky's breakup. Still, Connie's boobs are bigger than Patti Chan's, and she's on the next page, so she's not a total loser, and I guess Wayne likes them okay.

In real life, Frankie would never have touched me, or let me touch him, so maybe what happened doesn't really count.

Patti Chan and Tom Mummer, who met on the set of *Bigger Fools Than This*, had so much fun that they hope to appear in another movie together someday. They're expecting a baby next month, so you'd think her boobs would be bigger than Connie's by now, but they're not. Serena is hoping for a big jump in that department herself.

Nobody touches a piggy on purpose.

Patti and Tom are also looking forward to their wedding. She's got a diamond on her finger the size of a corn muffin.

Mother finally comes out of her room. "Liz is on her way home." She shakes her head. "We've got to get that boy straightened out. Got to." She looks tired and old. When Lucinda Lave is Mother's age, will she still be seeing Ricky Dan?

"Go to bed, hon."

I go upstairs, taking *People* magazine with me. Maybe someday Frankie will be featured. Since I've known him practically forever, they might even interview *me.* I'll leave out the part about touching.

I open my box of smoky blue stationery.

Dear Nobody in Particular, I write. *Frankie touched*

me today. I press my hand against my face. When I'm really old, and somebody yells "Robin" right in my ear, will I remember who I am?

I go back to my piece of paper. *It wasn't exactly personal,* I write. *Frankie didn't know who I was.* He probably thought I was China or Janice, or just a pair of anonymous boobs.

I touched him back.

Twelve

Twelve

Dad's got the radio tuned to golden oldies, and every time the Supremes come on, which is just about every other song, he thinks he's Diana Ross and starts singing.

Nobody wants to hear a grown man *ooooo* along with "Baby Love."

The Supremes happened longer ago than I was born.

Dad picked me up after school to take me to the dentist. That's his official medical duty. Mother does my regular doctor; Dad does the dentist. They divided me up when I was little.

When the song's over, I watch Dad closely—sometimes he gets depressed when the music stops and he realizes he's in the car with me instead of a Supreme. He looks okay, though, so I proceed, clearing my throat. "Frankie went in the hospital Saturday night."

"Oh, really?"

"Too many drugs. But he's okay now." I look

carefully for signs that he knows about the parallel universe, but he just snorts.

"Drugs! Well, that figures—the little bastard." He turns his head toward me. "You stay away from him, you hear? Next he'll be offering *you* drugs."

"No he won't! Besides, Mother says—"

"Your mother hasn't got the common sense God gave a gnat on a good day." He shakes his head in disgust. "You listen to *me*, not her!"

"Okay, okay." I hurriedly point to the car we're about to hit.

"I see it, Robin!" he declares. "I know how to drive. Don't turn into your mother on me." He glares at the station wagon we almost clobbered. At least when Janice almost hits a car, she *knows* she's about to hit it and laughs and swerves at the last moment. With Dad, you never know when you're about to end up dead.

He starts *ooooo*-ing again, this time with Ruby and the Romantics.

Mrs. Jenkins stayed home for only two days. She does have a boyfriend—the divorced vice president of Greater Soaps and Deodorants. She's already transferred from sales and is moving in with him—in Albany! Mother's having a hard time twisting her brain around this. Mrs. Jenkins with a man? A vice-presidential man? A man with money?

"He must be fat and bald," she declares, leaning against the counter, getting ready to peel potatoes. She sips a Diet Pepsi, watching Dick cut up a chicken. "And ugly."

Along with China, Mother has taken over as

Frankie's drug monitor. China got rid of his beer and wine stash and emptied out his drug drawer, and Mother gives him a pep talk every evening. So far, so good.

"Of course Frankie knew his mother was up to something," she continues, picking up a spud and aiming the potato peeler. "She hardly ever came home anymore! But he only found out for sure last Friday night." We're having fried chicken and green beans, with mashed potatoes and gravy. I'm snapping the beans.

"An obvious psychological dependency," Mother says, finishing the potato and plopping it into a pot of water. She offers Dick a sip of her soda. "I mean, the day after he finds out, he eats a bag of drugs!" Dick's hands are full of chicken gunk, so he dips his head back and she pours in the Diet Pepsi. It dribbles down his chin, and they both laugh as she wipes it off with a napkin.

I love fried chicken, but Mother never fixes it because it's too fattening. Dick, though, says a little sin makes virtue sweeter—which I think means it's okay to eat fried chicken once in a while. When he finishes cutting everything up, he lets me mix salt and pepper into a bowl of flour, and I get to dip and coat a wing and a leg and drop them in the frying pan. Then he takes over, because grease is popping everywhere.

"It's a shame," Mother says, stripping another potato. She's disgusted with Mrs. Jenkins. "Imagine, shacking up with some *executive,* as your only child slips into drink and drugs!" She peers at me over her potato. "I'd never do that to *you,* Robin. I'd be right there."

Gee. Thanks.

She motions for me to put the beans into a pot of water.

We also found out that Frankie hasn't been working. No new jobs, and he blew the ones he had lined up. He never even showed for the underwear shoot, plus he lost the investment services commercial. Last week he even got fired from his bartending job at Raze. "All this has been going on," Mother exclaims, "and we didn't know a thing! A good boy, lost to drugs. How could it happen?"

She attacks another potato with the peeler. I think her psychological dependence theory is shaky. Frankie lost all his jobs before finding out about his mother's fat, ugly boyfriend. I don't know why he chugs so many substances.

"Liz says it's up to him to change. Like she's too busy, now that she's got a man with a *position,* to spend time with her son. Well, thanks so much, Mrs. Jenkins!" Mother drops the naked potato into the pot. "I read *The Dark Secrets That Shape Your Family's Life* and felt like I was reading about Liz. I tell you, that woman is sick."

"I've got a dark secret of my own," says Dick, grinning.

"Oh?" Mother lifts her eyebrows, smiling back.

He leans over and kisses her on the cheek. "It'll have to wait till after supper," he says, laughing. Mother snickers and pokes him in the side.

I hate it when parents think they're sexy.

"Feel this, babe. Cashmere."

I touch the thin silver sweater Frankie is holding out to me. It's as soft as a kitten's breath. That's what Flower says about a baby's skin, as well as her boyfriend's eyelid, in the song, "This Time." It's the title cut on *This Time Around,* her second CD. Dick loaned it to me. He's got all her music.

The eyelid thing is kind of icky, but since I'm going to be an aunt, I like the baby part okay. I wonder if Flower has a baby of her own. When I asked Dick, he just shrugged and said, "Dunno, honey," and finished cutting up a turnip. He was making vegetable stew.

Honey.

Frankie pulls the sweater on over his head, adjusts it, and studies the effect. His tummy makes it poke out a little. The sweater will probably look better when he puts on his pants. Right now, he's just wearing silky, pale orange Harbingers. He touches his stomach and frowns. "Shit. Gotta get back to the gym." He jerks the sweater off and dumps it onto the floor, then sits on his bed, head in his hands. I pick up the sweater. By the time I've folded it so it won't get all wrinkled, Frankie's lying on his back, his face turned away from me. Is he asleep?

He stopped working out, just like he stopped everything else, but his tummy is still really small. I guess a belly of any size, though, will make it harder to get to L.A.

I set the folded-up cashmere sweater on a chair. Frankie turns his head toward me and pats the mattress. "Sit down, babe."

I wait just a fraction of a second, then sit. He doesn't seem to remember touching me. He doesn't seem to remember that Saturday night at all. "I got wasted," is all he'll say about it. "Big fucking deal."

He scratches my lower back through my shirt. "Lie down a minute, would you?"

I lie back. The edge of my rear end touches his side. He looks at me, full of facial disturbances. "I'm done, babe."

"Done?"

"Finished. This whole fucking modeling and acting shit. Finished. I'm not getting anywhere. I'm getting exactly *no*where." He touches his stomach. "Feel it."

I reach and touch his bare stomach. Since he's lying down, it's really not sticking out at all. Mine is still as round under my jeans as a Moon Pie.

"I'm getting fat. Getting old."

"No, you're not!" I lean on my elbow. "You're just in a biscuit place!"

He half turns toward me. "What?"

I lie back and point toward my stomach. "Biscuit place."

He laughs and runs his hand over my tummy. His hand travels up and over and around my stomach. The spot between my legs wakes up. "Biscuit place," he says, smiling.

"It'll pass," I suggest, my voice tight. "For you, I mean."

I'm afraid to move my hips. I wish his hand would take a wider path on its next trip around the base of my tummy, but instead it pulls back, and Frankie lies down flat again. "Do me a favor, would you, babe?" His voice is quiet.

Maybe he'll want to take another tour. "Okay. What?"

He takes my hand and puts it on his *thing*, pulling it out of his Harbingers, and I stop breathing. Maybe he *does* remember that I touched it. He puts his hand on top of mine, just like he did before, and soon his penis is as big and stiff as a fat sausage; in a minute he's gasping and shuddering and my hand is a gushy mess.

"Thanks, babe," he says. His eyes are closed. "That

was nice." He pulls me to his chest and the faint odor of Flute fills my nose.

Then he's asleep.

I still haven't opened the letter that came yesterday from Melissa. The tangerine envelope has been wedged in my Spanish text since last night. What kind of words did she send? Grace words, probably. I'm sitting outside school under an oak tree, even though it's chilly and the ground is damp and I'm all alone. I've already eaten my lunch, except for the pear, which is balanced on my right knee.

I carefully pull the envelope out and set it on my other knee, then close my eyes. The tree trunk is as hard as a rock behind my head. What would Melissa think if she knew I'd touched Mr. Studly's *thing*?

"Hey, Robin!"

I grab the pear and letter as my eyes whip open. Tri sits down beside me, and my heart does a little flip. I rebalance everything. He's got on a bulky, dark green pullover, which makes his skin and hair look even more like butterscotch. He smells like fall, leaves and chilly wind. Has a girl ever touched his penis? Is it butterscotch, too?

"Not talking today? Or too busy channeling?"

I look down, embarrassed, then glance at his face. "How's Baby Boom?"

"Booming." He scrunches up his nose in a scowl. "Babies all day long, screaming. Working at the Boom is the best argument for contraception I've ever heard." He leans against the tree, looking up through the branches. Has anyone ever died of a butterscotch overdose?

"Um, look," he says, "I'm sorry I haven't—uh-oh."

I make a frantic grab for my pear as it tumbles off my knee again. Tri catches and holds it in his palm, smiling. "Thanks," I mumble, tucking it into my backpack. I settle against the tree and put the envelope back on my left knee. How can I like Tri so much, when I've gone and touched Frankie's *thing*?

"So what's in the envelope?" His eyebrows lift in a question.

"A letter from Melissa."

"Direct communication from the dead! What's she got to say?"

"I haven't read it yet."

"'Course not. Reading and writing aren't nearly as much fun as channeling." He leans back against the tree again, smiling, and closes his eyes. I chew on my thumbnail.

He glances at me. "What I started to say was . . . I'm sorry I haven't been saying hi much. I've been kind of busy with stuff. And my mom"—he shrugs—"Well, I've just been busy. But now I need your help with a secret mission."

I blink. "Mission?"

"It takes place this Saturday night and involves midnight channeling under the maple tree, plus the possible ingestion of Nutsie Boy cones."

"Huh?"

His eyes dart away and come back again. "Um, I'm kind of asking you out."

Out? I stare at him, silent. What's he mean by *out*?

He looks at the ground, then at me, his skin beginning to flush. "The mean aunt warned me about this."

"About what?" He didn't actually mean *out* out, did he?

His mouth twists to the side. "The stunned reaction to color mixing. If that's a problem—"

"Oh. No! It's just that—I mean, it's just . . ." I touched Frankie's *penis*! I look down, then back up. "The mixing's okay." What will Mother think? "I like butterscotch."

"Butterscotch?" He lifts his eyebrows uncertainly.

"Your *color*." Doesn't he know he's butterscotch?

He laughs—he almost has dimples, but not quite. "Butterscotch!" His hair is a sandy golden halo around his head. Does he know about the parallel universe of liars? If he knew where to look, could he see me there now, touching Frankie?

"Okay, I can live with that. So, do you, um . . ." He leans forward and concentrates on driving an acorn around the toe of his sneaker with a twig. "Do you want to go out?" He tries to roll the acorn up the side of his foot with the twig, but it rolls back down.

I clear my throat, then tap him on the arm, waiting for his eyes to find mine again. "Do you mean out like in, um, *out*?"

He blinks. "Like in what?"

"*Out*. Like when people go to the, um, movies or something." I watch his face closely, holding my breath. Everything I learn I'll pass on to my niece or nephew, I promise.

His eyes dart away, then rush back, laughing a little. "Well, yeah," he says, using the twig to successfully flip the acorn over his entire foot, scoring a touchdown. "That's the general idea. *Movie* out. Followed by channeling and Nutsie Boys, or a suitable substitute." He looks directly into my eyes, and I discover he's got faint, tiny freckles on his nose. "You're the weirdest person I've ever met, you know that?"

Weird? What does he mean by that?

He hesitates, then reaches to take my right hand. "Weird is good. I grew up on weird." He turns my hand over, balancing the acorn on my palm, holding my hand upright with his own.

What do I do now? Except for Frankie in the *thing* situation, nobody's ever taken my hand before. And what's with the acorn? I watch it wobble.

"The mean aunt will want to know about the parental color reaction. So, if we went out—as in *out*—would your folks greet me at the door with a handshake or a shotgun?"

The acorn rolls off. Tri keeps holding my hand up, though, as if I was balancing a piece of air. I try a little experiment, turning my palm over. To my surprise, his fingers curl around mine, like they fit or something. And mine curl back! He lowers both of them till they're resting against his leg. We're holding hands! But does this mean we're—*holding hands*?

"I live with my mother. She doesn't have a shotgun," I say. "Or a handgun or anything." She's fine with our black neighbors by now, plus her supervisor at work is African American, and she likes him okay. I look at Tri. Of all the colors sprinkled in the neighborhood, none is as beautiful as his.

"Anyway, you're taking *me* out, not her." The envelope dives to the ground. Maybe it's as surprised to hear these words as I am.

The uncertainty in his face relaxes a bit, and he kind of laughs. "You're right about that, pie girl." He picks up the envelope and touches it to my nose. "I guarantee I can handle any and all evil spirits we encounter, not to mention oogie-boogies. Not every guy can say that. So, you wanna go channeling?"

My hand is still cupped in his. Can he sense its history of gush?

"Yes," I say, wadding my other hand into a fist and sticking it in my pocket. "I wanna."

Thirteen

Mother's on the phone with Frankie, checking how his day went. I could have told her. Up at noon. Gym. Home. Sleep. At least the gym's in there.

"Frankie," Mother exclaims, phone pressed between her shoulder and her ear as she opens up a jar of Papa Pito's Deluxe Spaghetti Sauce with Garlic, "you've got to believe in yourself! You'll get jobs again, and good ones! Just stay away from the drugs. Don't even *think* about them!" She dumps the sauce into a pan and turns up the flame. "Tomorrow I want you to get on the phone and talk to your agent. Tell him you hit a rough spot but you're okay now. You're a *terrific* model and a great actor. Everybody knows that! We all go through bad times now and then. You'll do swell!"

She's doing dinner in a hurry. It's mostly for me—quickie Italian, no meatballs—as she has to run out to a dress shop called B & B, which stands for Belles and Bells.

You can see why they just use the initials. She went there yesterday after work and found a dress that they're holding for her—tonight China's going along to help her decide if it's really the right one.

The water in the big saucepan comes to a boil, so I open the box of angel-hair pasta and dump it in. The water roils as I push the noodles under with a fork. Then Mother reaches in and takes over, waving me out of the kitchen, still talking to Frankie. She's always convinced I'm going to boil myself to death.

In the living room I turn on *Citizens' Round One.* Sometimes when John Johnson gets *really* mad, he practically spits. He breaks to a commercial, so I hit the remote and pull out Melissa's letter. It feels pretty skinny. It's probably all about Grace.

When words are all alone in an envelope—before someone takes them out to read them—do they even know they're words? Do they think about becoming sentences? I slide my finger under the flap.

No tweets, no cheeps. Wherefore why not, birdie girl? I rang the ring ring ringer-rang, we talked a Sunday morning talk, but still no peeps no whirly-words, no nothing from the tweeter girl.

Lost we us to far away?

She's signed it, *Mobilemess.*

I turn up the volume on John Johnson, except it's still a commercial, so I mute it again. I dig my box of stationery and my purple Lizard pen out of my backpack. *Dear Melissa,* I write, then stop. Can she see me lying on Frankie's bed, making his penis get big, then go all gushy? Can she see this, while she sits with Grace under special Alabama trees?

I scratch out what I've written.

Mother and China are giddy when they get home. It's the right dress! They don't have it with them, though, as it has to be altered. They both describe it in an excited rush, as if they've just discovered the cure for cancer. I hear "burnt peach," and "satin," and "fitted bodice," and "scalloped hem," and "short."

Mother charges off to call Dick. China sits on the other end of the couch and smiles at me. Her honey-blond hair cascades in waves to her shoulders, gleaming. She smells like flowers.

I know I'm supposed to say something, but what? Can she see me and Janice in the parallel universe, both of us touching Frankie's *thing*?

She clears her throat. "So how—"

"Somebody asked me out," I blurt.

"Really?" She grins, and when she does, she's prettier than Janice, probably prettier than everyone in the universe. Why can't Frankie be content? "Robbie, that's terrific! Who is it?"

I shrug. "A boy at school."

She laughs. "A boy at school! So *who,* silly?"

"His name is—"

"I left a message on Dick's answering machine. I completely forgot that this is his poker night. I tell you, being engaged is exhausting!" Mother laughs and plops down onto the couch, forcing me to slide closer to China.

China stretches her arms over her head and yawns, her breasts traveling upward, then back down with her arms. "I'd better get going. I told Frankie I wouldn't be late. We rented *Tommy's Run.* It's supposed to be terrific." Staying home and watching PG-13 movies instead of going clubbing in D.C. is part of Frankie's drug prevention plan. Mother's idea.

China kisses me on the top of my head. "I want to hear all about your date, okay?" She grabs her jacket and heads for the door. "Talk to you later, Claire." Then she's gone.

Mother sighs. "What a great kid. I'm so glad she's with Frankie. And she *really* knows clothes. Without her—" She blinks and looks at me. "Date?"

I slide farther down the couch. *"Out."*

"Huh?" Her hair looks like two o'clock in the morning, and her lipstick's gone.

"A boy asked me out."

"Out?"

"Out." Is that so hard to understand?

She runs her fingers through her hair, trying to fluff it back to life. Her nails are painted Rosie Blush—the same color as her missing lipstick. "What do you mean by *out*?"

Serena finishes the second-to-last blueberry muffin. "These are great. Where'd your mom get them?" She's wearing jeans and a blue plaid maternity blouse with a white collar. The blouse is pretty ugly.

"Green's," I answer, eyeing the last muffin.

"Mind?"

I shake my head no as Serena picks up the final muffin and bites. Since tonight is my first *out* event, I'm on calorie alert. I've got about eight more hours to lose weight. Still, it would have been nice to have something *blueberry* to eat later on.

Mother and Serena are going to Baby Boom to look at cribs. That might be more of my college money. Now that Mother has decided it's okay to be a grandmother, she wants to *buy stuff* for the baby. I didn't tell them that Tri works at the Boom. I also didn't mention that he's butterscotch. Why make everybody nervous ahead of time?

Besides, what if he changes his mind and doesn't show up?

I didn't tell Dad anything, either. Not even that I'm going *out*. It's hard enough dealing with Mother.

She strides into the kitchen in her fitted black pantsuit and red lips. She'll be back by the time Tri gets here, of course.

Serena wipes crumbs off her mouth and stands up. There's no hope when a pregnant woman takes over a plate of muffins.

I'm glad for her and the baby, but sometimes I wish it was just her and me again, going to a yard sale. Serena likes to rummage through every single junky box, picking up each dusty and cracked knickknack that catches her eye. Sometimes we laugh, like the time we found the tiny black-and-white corn-on-the-cob holders shaped like cows. Sometimes, though—like when she held an old chipped crystal up to the light and a rainbow of red, blue, and yellow flowed out the other side—we find something beautiful.

I head next door to water the plants.

* * *

I hear water running in the pipes, so I guess Frankie's in the shower. He's awake a little earlier than usual—it's only eleven-fifteen. He bartended last night for the first time since he messed up—Raze took him back! So you'd think he'd be down till at least one. But I know he's trying to get back in shape—he has to be able to *rise and shine*, to go on modeling jobs.

The dollhouse looks fresh and clean, like someone just went through it with a tiny Dustbuster.

In the dining room, three African violets are parched. In apology, I offer them jumbo gulps.

Frankie walks into the dining room, a towel wrapped around his waist, rubbing his head with a second towel. An incredible odor of *clean* comes with him—soap, hot water, a lacing of Flute. He combs his hair, slick and wet, back with his fingers. "I got a job lined up."

"Great. Where?" I pick up the watering can and head for his old bedroom and the geranium.

Frankie follows me. "It's a jeans ad, for Wayout."

Wayout. Not great, but not total loser. I glance at his belly. Except it isn't really a *belly* anymore. I guess starting to work out again and not drinking did it. It kind of disgusts me that it took such a short time. Maybe if I *started* drinking, then stopped, I'd lose weight.

The geranium looks depressed. "Has it ever faced the other direction?" I ask.

"What other direction?" Frankie's leaning against the door frame. He almost looks like Mr. Studly again.

"You know, turned around." I could try to rotate it, like I did before, only this time really do it. It'll be Thanksgiving in a month, and that might give it something to be grateful for.

"Who cares what direction it's facing?" Frankie drapes his hair-drying towel around his neck.

I turn to study the geranium. "The back part might be lonely for the sun."

I hear the floor creak, then feel Frankie's hands on my shoulders. He turns me around. "Forget the damn plant, okay? Listen, babe—China says you're going out tonight."

Is he laughing at me? Does he think that piggies don't go *out*? But his face is serious. I'm wearing sweats, but standing this close, and smelling him, makes me feel like I'm wearing only a towel, just like him. Or maybe the pink silky nightgown he and China gave me.

"Well? So what's the deal?"

"We're going to see *Twist Slip*." All these cops start getting killed by another cop, except either the bunch of cops or the cop killer might really just be virtual cops, but no one exactly knows. Mother frowned when I told her, but she didn't say too much. I think she's shocked that somebody actually asked me *out*.

"This the guy who drove you home late that time?"

"Yes."

Frankie puts his finger under my chin. "You know about safe sex?"

Safe *sex*? I pull my chin off his finger. "We're just going to a movie."

He laughs and kisses me on the forehead. "Dream on, babe." He puts his arm around my shoulder. "Come on. I'll give you some stuff." He walks me out of the room.

We go downstairs to his apartment, and I wait while he opens a drawer. "Here." He dumps about six little packages into my hands, all with different-colored wrappers. *Condoms.* Even *I* know what they are. They slide out of my hands onto the floor. "Oh, hell. Stick them in here." He holds a sock and I stuff them in. He laughs, looking at the slightly bulging material.

I stare at the sock. What am I supposed to do with it? I've seen Frankie put on a condom before, but that was looking through the window, long-distance. "Uh . . . ?"

He smiles. "Here, babe. I'll show you." He guides my hand to his penis, soft and still slightly damp from the shower, the towel falling to the floor. Then he closes his eyes, murmuring, "Nice," as I stroke. It gets bigger.

He walks me to the bed, where he gently pushes me back, pulls my sweatshirt off, and undoes my bra. My breasts are out! I want to hide them, but he smiles dreamily and takes them in his hands, then in his mouth. They've never been touched before. My nipples turn into hard buttons under his tongue. I don't want him to stop! But he does, sitting up and pulling out a condom. He shows me how to roll it on. "See, babe?" I touch him a while as he leans back, eyes shut. Then he rolls the condom back off and slides my sweats down my legs and off. Now he can see all my piggyness!

He smiles, opening my mouth with his tongue. It tastes like toothpaste and, I don't know, meat. A sweet, wet *Frankie* meat. Then he kisses my breasts, pushing his hands under my underwear to squeeze my rear end. He starts rubbing his *thing* against my belly, and my legs open on their own, as if they've been programmed to do this. I lift my pelvis and he shifts to rub his penis against my privates through my underpants, and I rub back—it's like we're giving each other a massage. Even my toes can't believe how good this feels—they don't want it to stop.

Then something starts to melt inside me. It feels small and delicious, like when your tongue finds a chocolate chip in a chocolate chip cookie.

Then it's a whole mouthful of chocolate chips.

Frankie shifts and rubs fast against my belly, finally convulsing and sending gush all over my tummy. Perspiring, moving in a kind of slow motion, he kisses the tips of my breasts, then rolls off and lies beside me. "Nice, babe," he says, his eyes blinking shut.

My eyes close, too.

Fourteen

Mother told Dad I'm going out tonight! I can't believe it. Now they're having a big fight over the phone.

"Brad," Mother says, "of course she's old enough! . . . No, I haven't met him yet, but . . . Don't be ridiculous! Robin knows how to behave. . . . No—he's seventeen. . . . Of course he's driving! . . . Honestly . . . All right, all right!" She slams down the receiver.

Serena sits at the kitchen counter, pretending she's reading the promotional material for Zen Cribs that she brought back from Baby Boom. She's having dinner with us and is spending the night, since Todd is out with a buddy. She has exchanged her plaid maternity blouse for a huge white T-shirt that has *Master's Piece* written across the front of it, over the stomach. I guess that's supposed to be funny.

"Your father—" Mother clinches her eyes shut, then shakes her head. "He *insists* on coming over to meet this Tri boy. As if I don't know how to raise my own daughter!" She's wearing jeans and a tight purple cardigan.

"Pizza!" Dick walks in through the side door, carrying a big flat box. When he called to suggest it, pizza sounded like a good idea. Now it sounds like piggy food plus garlic breath. I haven't lost any weight at all since this morning.

Mother scrunches her purple shoulders together and purrs as Dick kisses her on the back of the neck. "Here you go, Serena," he says, sliding the pizza across the counter and giving her a big smile. "Half plain, just like the pregnant lady ordered."

Serena laughs. Her face lights up whenever someone mentions the baby.

Mother gets out plates and napkins and sodas and we head for the living room. An old *Star Trek: The Next Generation* is on, and Mother and Dick think this is hot. "Brad's coming over," Mother tells Dick, as we settle on the couch, Serena taking the recliner. "As if he needs to *inspect* Robin's date! As if *I'm* incapable!"

"Well," Dick says. He smiles and gives me a wink, then dives for the pepperoni side of the pizza. Mother follows, so I take a plain piece. That's less calories, right? Plus Serena won't feel like the only plain person in the room. I check my watch. In ten minutes, I have to leave Captain Picard and go get ready. I've already had a bath—but what if Tri can still smell Frankie on me? I don't think it's a good idea to smell like somebody else on your first date.

Mother and Serena and China are rooting through my closet and drawers, deciding what I should wear. Each of them took one look at my long-sleeved pink T-shirt and made a face. Even *Serena* made a face. What's wrong with it?

"Honey," Mother says, "it just doesn't become you."

Tri liked it. *Nice shirt,* he said. I look down at my pink-covered breasts. My waist doesn't exactly go *in,* like it's supposed to. It sort of goes out. Can I help it that I didn't lose any weight today?

Serena finds my lilac blouse. "This is nice," she suggests. I *hate* my lilac blouse. I've hated it for two years. It's got *ruffles.* It makes me look like a piggy going to church.

"Robbie, what about this?" China—who frankly wasn't even invited, but just showed *up*—pulls a dark, midnight blue, velvety sweater out of my drawer. "It's lovely." She's wearing a slinky, low-cut silver dress. Frankie's off tonight, so he's taking her to dinner at Dodges. I guess if they go there early enough it doesn't count as clubbing.

The sweater she's holding has been in my drawer since last Christmas. Janice gave it to me. "I thought it would be a good, slenderizing color for you," she said, giving me a toothpaste smile. She didn't say anything about the leather key chain I gave her that had a small brass *J* on it, with fancy squiggles. She's also never used it. No way I'm wearing her stupid sweater.

"That's nice," Serena chimes in.

Mother holds it up, feeling the material between her fingers. "This might work. Janice gave it to you, didn't she? Try it on."

I'm not going to change with three people staring at me. I go down the hall to the bathroom. It's awful when grown women get ahold of you.

* * *

Dear Melissa. I'm sitting in a chair with my back to the dresser, just thinking a letter. I can't actually get out my purple Lizard pen and write one—I'm busy getting ready. China drapes one of Mother's thin gold chains around my neck, hooks a matching one at my wrist, then dots the back of my earlobes with perfume. It's called Raptured Star and smells just like she does—she had a tiny container in her purse.

I brushed my teeth three times, but I still smell like garlic.

China rummages through my box of Bad Girl makeup, plus the Forever bag that Frankie gave me over a year ago, and settles on a long, skinny tube of lipstick called Pink's Passion. She runs it over my lips. Mother nods approvingly, as Serena reclines on my bed and smiles. Maybe she's thinking about the baby's first date. On *her* first date with Todd, they went to a computer show. Figures.

Have you been on an Alabama date? Melissa probably just hangs with Grace. Is Grace tall like she is? Or short like me? *Have you ever touched somebody's thing?*

"There!" China says, standing me up and turning me toward the mirror above my dresser. A girl looks back. She's wearing a dark blue velvety sweater and jeans. Her plain brown hair comes down to her shoulders. Around her neck is a thin gold chain, glinting against the sweater, and her lips are painted pink.

She's still a chunk.

Bing-bong! Bing-bong! "That's your father," Mother says, shaking her head. "I'd better go down." She kisses me on the forehead. "You look nice, honey. Isn't it great to have China around?"

I put the lipstick in China's purse—she loaned it to

me, dumping her stuff into one of Mother's empty evening bags. It's leather, black, and tiny, with a long, skinny shoulder strap.

I hear Janice's voice—she came with Dad! Now she'll see me in her sweater. We're all here. Me and China and Janice. Two of us criminals. I start to sweat.

When I go down the steps, Dad turns and looks me over. Maybe he thought I'd turn into a Supreme or something for my first date, but I'm still me. His face is stern. "Robin—" he begins, but Mother interrupts.

"Brad, she knows how to act." She rolls her eyes at Janice, who smiles back. For once they have something to agree on—that, despite his bimbo habit, Dad's a prude. Though I guess Janice doesn't think of herself as a bimbo habit—she *is* his wife. She's wearing pressed jeans and a red pullover, her dark hair shiny and straight.

"I want her home by ten-thirty."

"Brad, I already told her eleven-thirty."

He glares at Mother. She purses her mouth, crossing her arms and jutting one hip out at an angle. I bet she and Dad didn't come home at ten-thirty on *their* first date.

She keeps her payback-time-for-leaving-me glare fixed on Dad a moment longer, then turns to me. "What time did you say the movie lets out?"

I didn't. "Um. Quarter to ten, or something. I guess." It starts at 8:05. I'm trying not to talk too much, so my lipstick doesn't wear off. How often are you supposed to put more on?

"Okay, then, eleven."

Dad sniffs loudly. "All right, eleven." He sits down on the couch next to Janice. That's when I realize all these people are still going to be sitting here when Tri arrives.

My tummy cramps, like I have to go to the bathroom. I thought everyone would disappear, or at least go in the kitchen. But Serena's back in the recliner, her short hair looking like a Grade 4 hurricane again. Dick's on the other end of the couch, sipping a can of Pepsi. Janice is in the middle, Dad at this end. Mother turns on her heel to cross the room and perch on the arm of the sofa next to Dick. China walks over and leans against the back of the recliner. Everyone looks at me. Dad's glaring, but everyone else is smiling.

I want to throw up.

Bing-bong! Bing-bong! Nobody says anything or moves.

"Hello! You must be—" Mother's standing in front of the opened door, her voice disappearing. I guess she just discovered the color mixing. She tries again. "You must be, um, Tri. Well, come in. I'm Mrs. Davis, Robin's mother." She's using her determined, "I'm okay with this, really," voice. She sounds only a little strained.

Tri is wearing a bulky, dark blue zip-up nylon jacket, and his hair is a sandy, radiant bush that fans out like it's trying to touch all the corners of the room at once. "Come in," Mother repeats—even though he's already in.

Tri looks at me and grins, raising his eyebrows. "Hey, Robin," he says.

"Hey," I reply, except it comes out squeaky.

Dad stands up, frowning, and clears his throat. "Hello, young man." He extends his hand and Tri takes it. "I'm Mr. Davis, Robin's dad." He clears his throat again. "So, ah, you two go to the same school?"

Tri nods.

"Yes," I say, but nobody looks at me.

"So, ah, you live around here?" Watching Dad's face, I can tell he's adding up Tri like a column of numbers. The color mixing is in the column, but it's not the only thing he's looking at. Class, background, family income, grade point average, college choice—*earning potential.*

"Over on Stanton," Tri answers, his eyes traveling over to me, then moving back to Dad. "Where Melissa used to live." He smiles at my mother.

"Melissa?" Then Dad seems to remember. "Oh. Yes. Well, I understand you're seeing a movie."

Tri nods. "Yeah. *Twist Slip.*" He discovers Janice sitting on the couch and raises his eyebrows in surprise, giving her a small wave with his hand. She flashes him a toothpaste smile.

"We've met," she explains, as everyone turns to look at her.

"Oh?" says Dad. He's already suspicious. So why doesn't he know about the parallel universe?

"At Baby Boom. When Robin and I bought the quilt for Kelly." She focuses her smile on him again. "You still working there?"

"Um, yes," says Tri. My first date—stun-gunned by my stepmother.

"We were at Baby Boom just today!" exclaims Mother. Then, "Heavens, where are my manners? Tri, this is my fiancé, Dick Pennington, and this is my daughter-in-law, Serena. And this is my good friend China. Everyone—Tri!"

"Hi, Tri," says China, smiling, her eyebrows lifted in approval. She steps from behind the recliner and walks across the room, her breasts moving freely under her dress, as slinky as the material. I glance at Tri and see that her breasts are cresting like silver waves in his eyes. She holds her hand out, and he finally remembers he has one, too. They shake.

"It's great to meet you," she says. She's as tall as he is. He could lift his hands and cup her breasts without moving anything else. "I hear *Twist Slip* is terrific. I hope you enjoy it." She probably means it, too. Like Serena, she's *nice.* Unlike Janice, she wouldn't cross a room just to start a tidal wave. She'd cross it for a reason—in this case, to say hi to Tri. It stinks when good-looking people aren't creeps.

"Uh," Tri says. I can tell he doesn't know where to look. I study the floor so I don't have to watch him faint from an overdose of airborne sex. Why go out with me when he can just stand in my living room with Janice and China and sniff?

"Well, you two better get going. Robbie, where's your jacket?" China's my date den mother.

Mother hands me my coat as Dad says to Tri, "She has to be back by ten-thirty."

"Eleven," says Mother.

Dad sniffs. "Eleven."

"Uh, okay," says Tri, as if he's just remembered why he's here.

China rolls her eyes pointedly at me. This is my date tip: *move.*

"We're going," I say, glad to get Tri out of the sex den. "Bye." I practically push him out the door. When it shuts behind us, we stand for a moment in the cold air, blinking, then start to walk down the sidewalk to his car. Maybe the chill will take the scent of China and Janice out of his nose.

He stops and laughs. "What was *that*?"

"What was what?" His breath makes fog. His hair is like a butterscotch mist rising from his head. I want to bury my face in it.

"Those people."

I frown. *Those people?* What does he mean by that? "Just my family. Plus China."

Tri looks at me. "Whew. Some family. I thought *mine* was weird. They always travel in a pack like that?"

Only to the parallel universe.

I climb into his car and just about break my arm trying to pull the seat belt out far enough to click it shut. It keeps sticking, making me start over. I hate being a fatso! Someone like me just can't compete with China and Janice. I wish he'd never met any of *those people.* I keep fumbling with the belt. When he leans over to help, we bang heads.

"Ow!" He rubs his forehead, glancing at me ruefully. "It's obvious that bugaboos and evil spirits are on the prowl. We'll have to be extra careful." He starts the engine. "Full speed or half? We don't want to wake the oogie-boogies."

I press my head where we bumped. Maybe I have some of his skin molecules on me now. "Full."

"All right! Let the channeling begin."

We take off.

Fifteen

All my lipstick disappeared during the movie. I lean closer to the mirror in the rest room, trying to ignore the tons of girls who are attempting to elbow their way to the sinks, and run the tube of Pink's Passion over my lips. Now it's on too thick. I rub it with my fingers. Now it's too thin—you can hardly see it. I aim the tube again.

"'Scuse me," says this girl, staring at me in the mirror. Her hair is bleached blond, sticking up and spiky, her lips some dark purply color. I'm surrounded by bodies. There's nowhere for me to move. Like she needs this spot more than I do?

"I have to wash my hands," she says. She's got black lines drawn around her eyes, and bunches of mascara.

Why did this stupid theater put their mirrors over the sinks? Nobody needs a mirror to wash their hands in. Didn't anyone consider the problems of lipstick management?

"Like now," the spiky girl says. She's got a nose ring.

I take a fast swipe at my lips. Too thick again. "Okay, okay," I answer. I blot my mouth on the back of my hand and she practically butts me out of the way with her skinny hip. I shove back with mine and she glares at me in the mirror, turning the water on really hard so it splashes. Since when are punk people so, you know, *clean*?

I take a last look at my lips, then grab a paper towel. I've got as much lipstick on my hand and fingers as I do on my mouth. The spiky girl strides past me, dumping her own paper towels in the trash. She gives me this look that says, *Piggy.*

Punk.

"No," Tri says. "The blond guy with the bright green eyes—Lieutenant Spiff Daniels, right? He was virtual, too. See, the whole thing was like this dream. Everything keeps going on forever the same way it always has. Like the universe or something. Then everyone starts realizing it's just a dream. Nothing's real, and if nobody wakes up, the unreal nothing will go on forever. So—shoot."

He wipes a dollop of soft ice cream off his jacket. He's got a sundae with chocolate fudge sauce and nuts; I've got a vanilla cone dipped in butterscotch. I love soft ice cream. We're sitting in his car outside the Moo Palace. There were no seats left inside, as all the booths and tables were jammed with kids. That's okay. I saw the spiky girl, along with another spiky girl—this one had *black* hair—and a spiky boy come in. I never realized that punk people ate ice cream.

"I thought Spiff was the real guy." I bite into the thin butterscotch coating and at the same time sneak my window down just a pinch. The heat's running—what if we end up dead from carbon monoxide poisoning? It could happen.

"Well." Tri digs his spoon into his sundae. "I don't think so. They did it like a puzzle, though, or a maze, so you're never really sure. I think the real guy was the black cop—Tad. He figured out the puzzle. At least, he was the one who concluded that they were *all* virtual."

"But that means he was virtual, too."

"Yeah, but his conscious realization of that makes him real. Don't you think?"

"Um." I lick my cone where I've bitten off a piece of coating. "Sometimes I think my brother is virtual. And his name sounds a lot like Tad—Todd."

"Yeah?" He laughs. "My uncle's name is Ted."

"Ted?" That doesn't sound very black. "He must like the ocean a lot."

Tri waves a spoonful of fudge sauce under my nose. My mouth opens like a baby's. He sticks the spoon inside, and I get a nut with it.

He takes a bite for himself. "Um. The ocean?"

"You know. Ted Beach."

"What's that got to do with the ocean?"

"Beach."

"Oh!" He laughs, scraping his cup of ice cream. "It's *Beech.* B-e-e-c-h." He licks his spoon. "As in, a robin bird singing in a beech tree."

"Oh." My face burns. How could I mistake geography for plant life? A drip of vanilla cream slides down my cone and I catch it with my tongue. "Is your uncle like your aunt?"

He wipes his mouth with a napkin and laughs.

"Not really. For one thing, he's a guy."

I giggle. "No, I mean . . ." I wrap a napkin around the bottom of my cone. It's beginning to collapse. "Is he black, too?"

He sets his almost empty sundae cup on the dashboard. "Pretty much." He looks at me, the light from the Moo Palace making his eyes gleam. "Why do you ask?"

"Oh. No reason." My cone cracks apart in my hands. Tri grabs his sundae cup again and shoves it under what's left of my cone. It avalanches, landing in drippy pieces. I *hate* it when that happens. I wasn't even finished. Tri hands me a bunch of napkins.

"Except?" He sits back and clears his throat.

I sniff, blotting my face with a napkin. I really think ice cream makes my nose run. "Except what?"

"There's always a reason people ask about race," he says, quietly. He waits, as if expecting an answer.

"Oh. Well." I wipe my hands on the rest of the napkins, not looking at him. "I was just, you know, wondering." I look at him. "I didn't mean anything."

His mouth twists in a slight smile. "Not meaning anything always means you mean *everything*."

"No, it doesn't! I just wondered if he was, you know—*black*. As in, uh, African American." Maybe that sounds better.

He sniffs. "Yeah, he's that, all right. The authentic real thing." He stares at me and I can't read his face. "So it's important?"

"No! I mean . . ." I dive into China's purse and pull out Pink's Passion. Why don't I have a compact or something? I yank down the visor over the passenger seat. Thank goodness—a mirror. I can just see my lips in the dim light. I open the tube and take aim, and it slips from my fingers, falling to the floor. "I, uh—" I dive forward, the napkins avalanching off my lap as I grope blindly in the dark.

"What are you *doing*?"

"Looking for my lipstick!"

Tri leans forward and reaches down between my feet, and I sit back, trying not to let tears spill down my face.

"Well, here it is."

"Thank you." My voice comes out strangled. The stick is slightly lopsided and coated with dirt, so I straighten it, hoping Tri can't see my face. The lipstick must be made out of plastic or something, because it doesn't break, and I wind it back down into the tube. The spiky girl was right. Piggies are the stupidest people in the world.

He sighs. "Could we back up and start over?"

I burst into tears.

"Man." He rubs his face with his hands. "Jeez!"

I try to wipe my face off. "It's just . . ." I dig in my jacket for a tissue. "It's just . . . your aunt's really black, and you're not, and I thought maybe your uncle wasn't either, but I don't care if he is, I just—"

"What do you mean, I'm not really black?"

"You're not. You're butterscotch!"

He stares at me, his mouth slightly open, then reaches to undo the emergency brake. "Well, excuse me, but I'm *plenty* black." His face is hard.

"Of course you are! I just meant—I mean . . ." He slams the car into reverse and starts to back up, and the engine jerks, shudders, and dies.

"Shit!"

We sit in silence. At least now I won't be asphyxiated, but maybe it's better to be a dead teenager than a live racist.

"I'm *black,*" he says. His voice is stretched thin and tight, like a wire that could slice you in half. "My father's white, since you're asking. But he's an asshole and I never see him. My mother's *black.* I live with my aunt and uncle, who are *black.* I've been *black* my entire life, so I think I qualify. Got it?"

I clutch the ruined tube of lipstick. "Yes."

The spiky girl leaves the Moo Palace with her spiky friends. They've all got cones dipped in chocolate. She doesn't need to lose any weight. She could eat twenty dipped cones every day. She'll go *out* again, too, every night of her life if she wants. After tonight, the only place I'll ever go is to the Quick Mart for Nutsie Boy cones, alone.

"I'm sorry." I put the lipstick back in China's purse. Tri is staring out the windshield, his mouth a hard knot. "What I said was stupid. And, you know, rude. I like you . . . I mean, the way you are. Butterscotch."

He shakes his head, his bushy hair dim in the dark. I never even got a chance to touch it. "Butterscotch," he repeats.

"Sometimes caramel. But mostly butterscotch."

He tilts his head to the side and looks at me. "Caramel?"

"Light caramel, except sometimes your eyes are dark caramel." Is he angry about his color? After all, he *is* mixed. He just said so. "I'm just giving you the facts."

He lowers his head to the steering wheel, and I hear something like a snort. "Facts," he says, except with his head down it sounds like *fax.*

He didn't say *fat,* did he?

When he sits up again, he's laughing. "Okay, fact number one: There are definitely evil spirits and bugaboos out tonight. Most definitely." He looks at his watch. "Fact number two: If my car doesn't start, you're going to be late—in which case, you'll find out real quick just how black I am."

I reach my hand out and touch his arm. "Thank you for *out,*" I say. "I'm sorry I ruined it."

"Out? Oh, yeah. *Out.*" He shrugs. "It's just . . ." He looks directly at me. "Don't tell me what I am. Or what I'm supposed to be. *Ever.* Just don't."

"Okay. I'm sorry. I won't."

He turns the key and the engine starts up without any problem. Tri pauses, engine idling, as he punches up a tape. A slow, deep music pours out—*black* music—a man's voice rising and falling, pleading for a lost love to return, his words a wet, gorgeous sorrow.

Bye, Moo Palace. Bye, spiky girl. Bye, *out.*

My street.

Tri hasn't said a word the whole way home.

As we pull close, I see Dad's car and Dick's car and Serena's car. Frankie's Probe sits red and glowing in his driveway. The lights are on in the house. Great. Everybody's home.

Tri stops the car and turns off the engine. The music disappears.

I undo my seat belt. I don't need a date den mother for *this* move. "I'll just jump out," I say. I grab the door handle. "Thanks."

"Well, wait a minute." Tri sighs and leans back, closing his eyes. "Okay, this is how I see it."

I blink. Tri's looking at me now, his face full of moonlight.

"We did it all wrong. We should have started out immediately with channeling. That way we could have warded off the evil spirits and bugaboos. As it was, we got bit in the butt, bad."

I almost stick my hand under my rear end to check, but don't.

"So. We have to start over."

What does he mean? "Go back to *Twist Slip*?"

"No, silly." He leans toward me. "You've got a piece of cone in your hair." I feel his fingers flick something away. "Plus melted ice cream." He rubs my head with the cuff of his jacket. Then his mouth is about ten inches away from mine, moving closer. I have to cross my eyes to see it.

His lips touch mine so softly I almost don't feel them. He pulls back and blinks, then leans forward again. This time, my lips touch back. I've never thought about how lips are kind of prehensile. Mine are still exploring when he pulls back again.

"Okay," he says, "but that's not really channeling."

"What?" We were channeling? Except not really?

He comes close. "This." Once more his lips touch mine, except this time something sweet comes through them, and his tongue is pushing gently into my mouth, and mine's touching back. He tastes like vanilla and chocolate and caramel, and something else. *Tri.* He tastes like Tri.

Garlic!

I pull back abruptly. "I had pizza for dinner!"

He clears his throat. "Yeah. I thought maybe so. That or spaghetti."

A piggy nightmare! I bet the spiky girl never has pizza breath!

He pulls my chin back. "But me big, strong man."

His lips touch mine again, and this time our tongues engage immediately in deep channeling. I think he's right about it warding off the—

Bang!

We jerk apart.

Someone's standing next to the car. Then Frankie's leaning down, rapping on my window.

"Frankie!" I bleat.

"Christ," Tri says, wiping his mouth.

"It's okay," I add, hurriedly. "He's my next-door neighbor. China's boyfriend."

Tri leans over me and fumbles for the window roller.

"Sorry to interrupt," Frankie says, smiling. "But Robin's dad is so uptight, China's afraid she'll get in trouble. She sent me over." He points to his glowing watch. 11:13!

"Okay," says Tri. "Right."

"See ya later." Frankie gives me a wink and walks back toward his house.

"What is this, the Neighborhood Watch?" Tri is pissed, I can tell.

"I better go in." I reach for China's purse. "I liked the channeling," I say. "I think it helped."

His anger disappears under a grin. "Definitely. *I* certainly feel better." Even though the light in the car is shadowy, everything brightens when he smiles.

We walk to the door, but before we even get there, it

swings open and my father is glaring at me. "It's eleven-fifteen, young lady!"

Standing behind him is Mother. "Honestly, Brad. Fifteen minutes!" She smiles at Tri. "So how was the movie?"

"Great," he says, smiling back. "Sorry we're late." He touches my arm. "Well, I gotta run. See you later."

Then he's gone and I'm inside staring at Mother and Dad and Janice and Dick. On a card table are the remains of an unfinished game of Monopoly, a big pile of money at one end. I know whose it is. When Dad plays, he always ends up owning every hotel in the solar system. At least Serena had the decency to go to bed.

Dick waves at me from the table and starts picking up the pieces and putting them away. Janice, sitting catty-corner from him, looks bored out of her mind.

"Well?" says Dad.

"Well, what?" He's adding me up like a column of numbers. Is Tri's tongue in the total?

"Brad, leave her alone! Fifteen minutes is nothing." She looks at me and I nod. I don't say anything about turning temporarily into a racist. I don't say anything about channeling.

She stares Dad down, and he finally gives up. "Okay, then." He turns to Janice. "You ready?" She is *so* ready.

Everyone mills around until Dad and Janice get their coats and finally leave. I go upstairs. It's too cold for my pink nightgown, the one Frankie and China gave me, but I put it on anyway, pulling a flannel gown over it. I dig out my purple Lizard pen.

Dear Melissa, I write, then stop.

Dear Nobody in Particular, Two different people kissed

me today. One is a butterscotch boy. I want to kiss him again, but he doesn't know that I live in the parallel universe.

I can feel the silky pinkness of the gown against my skin. Frankie's *thing* in my hands was silky, too—just like his tongue against my breasts.

Once you're in the parallel universe, can you ever get out?

Sixteen

Melissa's face floats toward me, her red curls stretching and undulating like a thousand wavy fingers. A curl brushes my face, like a harmless jellyfish tentacle. She's swimming in the greeny gulf, the top half of her naked, the tips of her small breasts a high, bright pink.

Whack! Right on my rear end! It's her mermy tail. She laughs and turns away, her skinny greenish white arms moving like strands of pale seaweed, motioning for me to follow. I swish my finny—

Whack!

"Robin! Would you wake up? I've been calling you all the way up the stairs!"

Huh?

I groan and roll over. Mother's standing above me in her black silk robe, a piece of newspaper folded in her hand, threatening to smack me again. "Honestly. You weren't out *that* late. Melissa's on the phone. Hurry up!" She unfolds the newspaper, shaking her head. "Now I've mashed up the sports section. Dick's gonna kill me." She turns to leave. "I'll tell her you're on the way, but *hurry*. She's long-distance."

I stare at the ceiling, trying to blink the greeny gulf out of my eyes. I thought salt water would sting, but—

Melissa! On the phone!

I roll out of bed, landing on my knees with a thud. Then I'm tearing out of my room, pushing past Mother on the steps, charging past Dick in the living room—he smiles at me vaguely as he rummages through the fat Sunday paper—and then I'm in the kitchen, grabbing the phone. I pause a moment as Mother's voice floats in from the living room. "I found the sports section," I hear her say. "I pulled it out by mistake with Arts." She doesn't say anything about mashing it.

"Hi." My voice sounds tinny. It's been so long since I was with Melissa—except it's only been a minute. We just went swimming!

"Hi." In the silence that follows, her voice glides through my head like an underwater current. "Why haven't you written me?" she asks.

"Melissa," I say, then stop. I don't know why I haven't written.

"Don't you like me anymore?" Her voice is tight, like cold water.

"Of course I do! But my letters are silly. I can't write like you."

Silence.

"If I wanted you to write like me, I'd send a letter to myself." Her voice is still tight.

"So how's Grace?" Might as well get right to it. I can make my voice hard, too.

"Grace?"

"The one who's teaching you to swim. Your mermy friend!" Does she think I'm stupid?

"My . . . what?"

"Your mermy—" I stop, my face flushing. "Um, nothing." No, when you say *nothing,* you mean *everything.* I fiddle with the buttons on my nightgown.

"Mermy friend?"

I notice Mother left a couple of sections of the newspaper sitting next to the coffeepot, so I pick up Arts and hug Movie Previews to my chest. "I, um, thought maybe Grace was teaching you to swim in the Gulf. You know, like a mermaid."

"Oh. I already know how to swim."

"Yes." I knew that.

"So, why—"

"I went out," I say.

"Out?"

"*Out.*"

"What do you mean?"

"*Out.*" Am I the only one who knows what *out* means? "You know . . . to the movies." She doesn't respond. "With a *boy.*"

"Boy?"

"The opposite sex!" Honestly.

"Well, I know what boys are." Silence. "Really?"

"Yeah." Take that, Grace. "Plus, we channeled."

"You what?"

Mother walks into the kitchen. "Seen the arts section?" She notices it mashed against my chest and holds her hand out, so I give it to her and she leaves.

I twist the phone cord in my fingers.

"You did what?"

Can't she hear? *"Channeled."* I look to make sure Mother didn't come back into the kitchen. "We, um, kissed. With our *tongues.*"

"Oh." She doesn't sound very excited.

"You don't sound very excited."

"Well, no. I mean, great. It's just that . . . I, um, haven't done that."

Maybe she thinks I'm bragging. "You will," I say. I picture a tall, skinny boy kissing her. He's got freckles, too, and a big proboscis just like she does, so they bump noses, but then she tilts her head and he makes a landing. "I didn't think anyone would ever—"

"We're coming up for Christmas."

"Really?"

"Yeah. But I'm not going to come see you if you aren't my friend anymore."

"Of course I'm your friend!" Is she crazy? We just went swimming!

"Then prove it! *Write.*" I hear an urgency in her voice. "If I don't get a letter from you by Wednesday, I'm never writing to you again, and I won't come see you. So there!" She slams down the phone.

Serena sits bundled up at the kitchen table in her shaggy robe, drinking herbal tea, while Mother, still poured into her black silky robe, sips coffee. Dick, already dressed, makes pancakes. The kitchen smells like IHOP.

After serving up a bunch of flapjacks to me and Mother and Serena, Dick lets me take over spooning batter onto the grill, watching for bubbles, flipping. Dick likes his pancakes with jelly. Ugh. The rest of us are syrup people.

There's some batter left. Afternoon snack! Pancakes heated up in the microwave and buttered and syruped. I spoon more onto the grill.

Todd walks in. He gives Serena a big hug and kiss and pats her stomach, laughing. He's pretty excited about the baby—I just hope it doesn't come with a keyboard attached. Then he pulls up a chair. So I'm supposed to serve him? He smiles as I hand over the last of the pancakes.

There seems to be some kind of truce going on between him and Dick. While Todd butters and syrups, Dick starts talking about what it was like when he had *his* children. Two boys, Brendan and Cliff. "Nothing like the smell of a baby," he says, smiling.

Max could get pretty stinky. I changed his diaper exactly twice. He squirted me the second time. I didn't think that was very funny, but Melissa couldn't stop laughing.

Dick holds his coffee mug as he talks. "For the first three months, Brendan cried from morning till night," he says, staring at the tabletop as if it is a crystal ball and he can see a squalling baby. "But he grew out of it."

He never says too much about his sons as adults, even though one is living with him due to the emergency job loss. Apparently they took their mother's side against him during the divorce, even though *she* was the one running around. His jaw gets real tight whenever the subject of cheating comes up.

I try not to think about the parallel universe.

While Todd and Dick have another cup of coffee, all

the females leave to get dressed. When we regroup, I've got my box of stationery and purple Lizard pen with me. I sit at the kitchen counter as Mother, changed into jeans and a bright pink sweatshirt, cleans up the dishes. Dick and Todd and Serena sit around the kitchen table and talk cribs and—this is pretty icky—breast-feeding. They all agree it's a good thing. Mother runs the water extra hard during this part of the conversation.

Dear Melissa, I write. This is it. I have to say something and mail it. *Todd and Serena are having a baby. They're happy, and so's Dick, who's now engaged to Mother. I saw* Twist Slip *with Tri last night. This was before we channeled. While he is light skinned, he is actually quite black. Dad and Janice are still together, even though she's a horny slut. Have you ever touched someone's thing? Well, that's all for now. I'm still your friend and really want to see you at Christmas. XOXO, sweet tweet Robin.*

I fold it up and seal it in a smoky blue envelope, then address it. It's Sunday, and she has to get it by Wednesday, so I'll have to walk to the post office and use the slot in the lobby. On the way back, I can detour to the Quick Mart for a Nutsie Boy.

I thought after you channeled with someone, he'd sit with you at lunch or something. But I've seen Tri only a couple of times, at a distance. Is he sorry that he did it with me?

It's been cold, so almost no one is outside except me. This one girl—Corinne—has been sitting next to me in Spanish, and she asked when I eat lunch, but we go at different times. She's in the Spanish club. I could join, too, if I wanted.

At least outside nobody will see me eat my stupid low-fat turkey sandwich and loser apple. Plus maybe the cold air will make me burn more calories.

I hope Melissa got my letter on time. Today is Thursday. Yesterday was the deadline.

I eat my apple down to the core, then look around to make sure no one is watching and toss it under a bush. Maybe a chilly ant or shivery bird will find it and be grateful. I open a Twinkie pack and split one down the middle, licking it out to make a boat. A *Mayflower* Twinkie! Thanksgiving is next week.

I sing "Gone Missing" to the geranium, from Flower's *Been There* CD. It's been running through my head all day. "'Why are tears all that's left in this lovin' you song?'"

The geranium's been droopy lately, the leaves turning yellow, so I'm hoping a little music will help, even though it's a sad song.

"'Can't take you going missing . . .'" I get my arms around the huge clay pot. "'Every time we get through kissing . . .'" I tighten my arms, heave, and spin slowly, not daring to stop. The pot weighs a ton, but I make it all the way around without dropping it and shove it back onto the windowsill. There!

It's in exactly the same position as before. How did that happen?

"What's with you and this plant?"

Frankie's frowning at me. He's wearing tight jeans and a thin dark pullover. For a minute, I think it's the same sweater I wore to *Twist Slip*. I pick geranium leaves off my chest. "It needs the sun," I say.

"It's got the sun."

"But not on both sides."

He sniffs. His mom and her boyfriend are coming down for Thanksgiving. I don't think Frankie's too happy about it.

"What does your mom's boyfriend look like?" I smell like a geranium. I've got potting soil on my shirt, so I brush it off.

He shrugs. "Roadkill. Why?"

"Just wondering." I look at Frankie's jeans, and the tips of my breasts start to feel tight. Does his mom think about her boyfriend's penis? "What do you think his thing looks like?"

"His what?"

I rub my arms. They ache a little. I don't know what to do about the geranium. When I took this job, I wasn't prepared for the slow death of plants.

"His *thing*."

"English?"

I point toward Frankie's privates.

He looks at me incredulously. "His *dick*?" His mouth tightens, his eyes a blue heat. He walks toward me and pulls my chin up with his fingers, his glare neon.

"That's sick. Don't say it again. Don't even think it."

His fingers are squeezing my chin. Even angry, his lips are curved and perfect. Then his fingers soften. The hot glare in his eyes cools. He brushes my hair back and runs his fingers over my face, then cups it with both hands. When his mouth touches mine—his tongue pushing its way inside—I forget about China.

* * *

We're lying on his old bed in the geranium room. He's naked. I'm still wearing my underpants, my tummy sticky with gush. We gave each other massages again. Now he's asleep. I poke him in the side until he wakes up.

"What?" His eyes open only halfway, so I poke again. He blinks at the ceiling, then scratches himself, letting his *thing* flop around.

"Shit, what time is it?" He has to work at Raze tonight. I have to go home for dinner.

He rolls off the bed, grabs his clothes, and heads for his apartment. I sit still a minute, then follow. By the time I get downstairs, I can already hear the shower running.

When he comes out, toweling off, I'm sitting on his bed, still wearing just my underpants. Maybe he'll want to touch me again. I shake my hair back so it looks sexy.

He stops toweling. "What are you doing? Get dressed."

He never says that to China or Janice. But they're not *fatsoes,* either. Who am I kidding?

Frankie tucks the towel around his waist and sits next to me. "What's up, babe? You look like you just lost your best friend."

I shrug. "I'm a piggy."

"Piggy?"

"Fat." I poke my tummy.

He smiles and places his hand on it, circling its roundness. "You've just got a little extra, that's all. You're fine."

I am? "Well, then how come you didn't put your *thing* in me?" He always puts it in China.

He laughs. "You mean screw?" He leans over and kisses me on the forehead, running his hand up from my stomach to cup my breast. He squeezes it gently, then stands up and walks to the mirror.

"Well?"

He combs his hair. "You want me to get arrested? Forget it. You're too young." He studies himself in the mirror. "We were just messing around. Save the big stuff for your boyfriend." He grabs my shirt and throws it at me. "Now get dressed, would you?"

I get dressed.

"Oh," he says, as I head for the stairway, "I heard your father's going out of town this weekend. Some kind of business trip."

I blink at him. Dad's going to Atlanta. "Where'd you hear that?"

He shrugs. "I think your mom mentioned it." He smiles at himself in the mirror.

Janice.

Seventeen

I hate going to the store when it's this crowded. Who needs a million people breathing down your neck when you're reaching for a pack of Oreos? Fortunately, I was able to grab one before six women roared up with their grocery carts.

The only item officially on my list is mushrooms.

The vegetables at Super Food aren't nearly as ritzy as the ones at Green's. But Green's is too far to walk to, so Mother will have to settle for middle-class mushrooms. She's making Dick beef Stroganoff tomorrow for dinner. It's their ten-month anniversary, so this dinner is a big hoo-ha.

There's two different kinds to choose from. Round grayish white ones, and big brown ones. I think she wants the light ones. But—prepackaged or loose? She didn't alert me to the mushroom perplexities.

"Hi, Robin *bir-r-r-d*!"

I whirl around. Becky Beech!

She giggles into her hand, her eyes dark and shiny. This is supposed to be funny? Then she turns and calls out to an African-American man in a black leather jacket, standing over by the potatoes. "Dad! It's Tri's *gir-r-rl-*friend!" Her father is tall and dark and skinny. I'm short and light and fat. I glare at her.

"Becky, shut up!" It's Tri, in his bulky nylon jacket, yelling from squash on the other side of broccoli. He starts over, holding a bag of zucchini.

"Why?" asks Becky. Her hair's in sideways cornrows or something. Shouldn't they be going front to back? "Isn't she your *gir-r-r-l*friend anymore?"

Tri reaches mushrooms and glares at her.

"Becky, get over here! Leave Tri alone." It's her father, still picking over potatoes. His jacket looks like leather, but it could be that fake stuff. He slides some spuds into a bag, then moves on to onions.

Tri waits till Becky is leaning against her father's arm, sticking out her tongue, then looks at me. "Hi," he says. His face isn't smiling.

"Hi." I guess I didn't channel very well. Plus, of course, the temporary racist situation.

"It's my aunt's birthday. I have to help my uncle cook." We stare at the mushroom display.

"Have you ever had—"

"I *hate* to cook," he blurts out, startling me. "It's Uncle Ted's day off, so he thinks this is a great idea. He's doing the barbecue and potato salad and I'm supposed to fry squash and make a fruit salad. *Nobody* eats fried squash on their birthday! Why can't he just take her out to dinner like everybody else?" He sniffs, then clears his throat. "I think I'm getting a stinking cold."

"Oh." We stand in a little pool of silence. "Have you ever had mushroom pie?"

He blinks and studies me a moment. "There's an idea. You inviting us over for dessert?"

Is he serious? "I'm not talking about *dessert* pie. I mean *quiche,* with eggs and vegetables and stuff. It's a pie you eat for *dinner.*" Dick made us one, once.

Tri sniffs again. "Okay."

What a grump. I open my mouth, then shut it. Peeking around his arm is Ray. So what vegetable does *he* have? A pineapple.

"Hi," he says, grinning.

"Hi," I say. "Nice pineapple."

He plucks a frond easily from the top of the prickly fruit and holds it up to my nose. "Smell it."

I sniff politely.

"It's ripe!" he exclaims, his grin triumphant. "It's my birthday present for Ma. She *loves* pineapple."

"Beat it," says Tri.

"So what did *you* get her?" Ray fixes him with hot eyes.

"Uncle Ted!" Tri's voice sounds like a bullhorn.

Uncle Ted lifts his eyes from the celery. "Ray, over here. *Now.*"

Tri fumbles for a tissue in his pocket and rubs it under his nose. "So," he says, glaring at Ray's back as Ray sashays over to his father, "you frying squash tonight, too?" He pockets the tissue and turns his gaze on me.

I start to laugh, but stop. His face isn't laughing back. "I'm buying mushrooms for my mother," I explain.

He's still staring at me. "I don't know what kind to get," I add. "I mean, the light ones, but prepackaged or loose?"

Tri picks up a package and examines it. "These look

kind of scummy." He gets me a plastic bag, and I start filling it up with loose ones. I'm supposed to get a lot.

"You doing anything Sunday afternoon?" he asks.

Huh? His eyes are focused on me like they're looking for something. I feel my face start to flush. "Sunday?"

"Yeah. It usually comes after Saturday, but occasionally, especially following intensive channeling, it comes the day before Monday."

I smile, and his face begins to relax. He shrugs. "Maybe we can ride out to Camden Lake or something."

Camden Lake! I know kids go there, but I've only ever been there with Mother, when she was dating a guy who liked picnics. It's small and man-made, but it *is* a lake—it's a lot bigger than a pond. You can rent canoes and stuff, but probably not at this time of year. "Sure," I say. Mother hasn't voiced any color-mixing concerns about Tri. I think she feels it's important to be modern.

He finally really smiles. "One o'clock okay?"

"Sure," I repeat, then look over his shoulder. Uh-oh. It's Uncle Ted, with the grocery basket.

"You must be Robin. I'm Tri's uncle," he says, extending his hand. I take it. He's older than he looked across the produce aisle. I think the leather jacket *is* fake—but it's a nice fake. Becky wiggles around behind him. I open my mouth, but nothing comes out.

"Tri said *Twist Slip* was pretty good," he offers.

"Um, yes." I look to Tri for backup, but he's busy whipping out a zucchini to sword-fight Ray, who's jabbing him with the pointy fronds of his pineapple.

"Tri, cut it out," Uncle Ted says. "And Ray, for the last time, put that thing in the cart!"

"The movie was terrific," I continue, watching Tri

slide the zucchini back into the bag. "I thought—*agh*." I grab for the pack of Oreos as it slips from under my arm. Too late. It lands on the floor with a smack, just as Ray dives for them.

"They're okay," he says, holding them up and examining them critically.

I take the package from him. There don't appear to be any casualties. I tuck them back under my arm. "Thanks."

"We can give you a ride home, if you like." Uncle Ted's voice is deep.

I blink. A ride? I glance at Tri, who seems as surprised as I am. He shrugs slightly and smiles. "Um, sure," I answer. "Thank you."

Uncle Ted takes the bag of zucchini from Tri's hand. "We'll meet you out front, then. Come on, kids." He pushes the basket toward checkout, Ray and Becky trailing, looking back over their shoulders and giggling.

"You'll need some milk with those Oreos," Tri suggests. I nod, and we head for Dairy.

I walk across the parking lot with Tri and the Beech bunch. It's weird. I want to smile and wave at everyone we pass, so they can see me being noble and integrated and everything. I also feel, I don't know, embarrassed and hope nobody notices me.

When we get to the car, Tri opens the back door on the passenger side and motions me in. Before he can follow, Ray and Becky turn into WWF TV wrestlers and dive in after me, thrashing around until I'm wedged between them. I get an elbow in my ribs and a knee in my stomach. "Sorry," says Becky, pushing herself into an upright position, panting.

We're Siamese triplets.

"You two—" Uncle Ted starts, but Tri exclaims, "Oh, forget it!" and dumps his bag in the backseat next to Ray, then climbs into the front. Before we take off, Uncle Ted turns on a radio sports show and a whole bunch of guys start screaming about basketball. Ray and Becky take turns popping gum in my ears.

When we pull up in front of my house, all I can smell is Double Bubble.

"Bye," says Tri. Does he remember that he asked me about Sunday afternoon?

"Nice meeting you," says Uncle Ted, looking at me in the rearview mirror, his eyes dark and unreadable.

Becky climbs over my lap so I can get out. I get another knee in my stomach. "Bye, Robin *bir-r-rd*!" She giggles.

"Thanks for the ride," I say, sliding out the door opposite Tri, clutching my bag of mushrooms and Oreos and milk.

Tri ducks his head so he can see me. "Sunday," he says, lifting his hand in a small wave. He smiles tensely as Becky and Ray shriek in unison, "Sunday!"

"You two be quiet!" Uncle Ted barks. They lapse into giggles.

I wave good-bye as they pull away. Ray waves back all the way down the street. He's the only one who does.

Dad left on his trip yesterday afternoon while I was buying mushrooms. He'll be back Monday. Frankie worked at Raze last night till really late, so that's one Janice-free night. Two more to go, Saturday and Sunday.

Mother's cutting up strips of beef for the Stroganoff.

"Tri's picking me up tomorrow afternoon," I say.

The knife pauses over a strip. "Oh?"

"We're going out."

"Out?"

"Out!" Can't she remember anything?

She looks at me. After her morning hair appointment, she's got poofed-up, shiny, *hot lady* hair.

"Where?"

"To Camden Lake. He's picking me up at one."

She sniffs and sets the knife down, then wipes her fingers off with a paper towel and reaches for a tissue. "I think I'm getting that darned cold that's going around."

Tri's cold!

"So," she says, "Tri's mixed-race?" I freeze. She looks at me. "So which is which?"

"Which is which what?"

She laughs and takes a sip of Diet Pepsi. "Which parent is black?" A smudge of Dark Lilac Rhapsody lipstick is left on the can.

"Um." I shrug as she picks up the knife again. "His mom. But I told you he lives with his aunt." Plus Uncle Ted and the girl-killing cousin-monsters.

"Hmm." She starts slicing again. "What happened to his parents?"

I don't know. "I don't know."

"Oh." She sniffs and clears her throat. "So his mother is the one who's black? Usually it's the other way around." The beef-slice pile is getting higher. "Just don't get too serious, honey. After all, Tri's only your first guy."

I hear the distant clang of the mailbox lid and make a fast exit.

I stare at the tangerine envelope. A letter from Melissa! It's postmarked Tuesday. Did my letter get there early? I go upstairs to my room. Mother has stopped slicing long enough to put on Aretha Franklin. She's singing along, probably dancing, too.

I open the letter.

Robin. Just that, no "*sweet tweet.*" *Mobilemess bestirs a dangerness. Maryland time once mine is gone gone gone away.*

Did she get my letter? She doesn't even mention it.

Write me write me tell me I am fine. The Gracie girl we sat one time beneath a bushy tree all full of smell. She kissed me kissed me kissed me but no more not even once but everything is dark and scared I'm running through a black black night no stars no moon it doesn't end please write me tell me tweeter girl I only dreamed please tell me tell me I am fine please write me write me write me.

Stunned, I sit quietly as my lungs empty. In the background, Aretha, lungs full, demands respect. Melissa kissed *Grace*? I take a big, noisy gulp of air. She kissed *Grace*?

Eighteen

1:20.

No Tri.

Mother's sucking a cherry cough drop as she sits on the couch, sorting laundry and watching *The Ghost and Mrs. Muir*. We've seen it about a billion times—she bought it a couple of years ago. I'm in the rocking chair in the corner, next to the bookcase, pretending to read *Clarkson's History of Ancient Greece*. Mother's never read it, either, but having it in the bookcase makes us look like we're intelligent. There's enough illustrations to demonstrate that Greek people hardly wore any clothes. You could probably tell right away if somebody had a boob job.

The scent of cherry makes it clear across the room.

Mother always cries at the end of the movie, when Mrs. Muir, grown old and wrinkled, finally dies and the sea captain ghost comes back for her and she's young and beautiful again and they go away to live together for eternity. I think Mother's hoping that will happen with her and Dick.

1:24.

Nobody helped me get dressed this time. I put on my long-sleeved pink tee. *Nice shirt*, Tri had said.

1:26.

Mother sniffs loudly and reaches for a tissue. She's probably glad I got stood up. No need to worry about which parent is which.

Bing-bong! Bing-bong!

"For Pete's sake, Robin—open the door!" Mother dumps my underwear and socks back into the laundry basket. "I told you not to worry."

I open it. Tri smiles apologetically. "Sorry I'm late. I was helping Ray with his homework and lost track of time." He coughs into his fist, then nods at Mother. "How you doing, Mrs. Davis?" His voice is a little hoarse.

"Just fine, Tri." She sneezes and Tri coughs again. "Except for this cold. Sounds like you've got it, too." She blots her nose daintily with another tissue, then flashes her old lady *hot* smile at him—she went with the Dark Lilac Rhapsody again. I left my lips blank. I didn't know what color other than Pink's Passion would look good, and that got destroyed. "Bundle up," says Mother. "It's nippy out."

I pull on my jacket, and we head out to get nipped.

We're sitting next to each other on top of a picnic table under a huge covered pavilion. Behind us, about a hundred picnic tables with attached benches are crowded together and chained one to the other. Why? Who would steal an entire picnic table? You'd have to tie it to the top of your car, and everyone would see you driving off.

It gets dark so early now, the afternoon is already disappearing. A few people are still around, but not many—some teenagers messing around on the pier, a couple of straggly families, and some loners. Mostly the place is big and empty.

I'm not cold—I've even unzipped my jacket—because we walked around the lake. *Twice.* Tri skipped stones across the surface. I tried, but mine all sank right away. He showed me how to hold my hand and arm, but it didn't work—they drowned immediately.

He ended up handing me sticks to throw. At least they *float.*

I rub at a damp spot on my jacket—I'm pretty sure it's lake juice. "Do you think mermaids only live in salt water?" I ask.

He raises his eyebrows at me. "Mermaids?"

"I mean . . . if they existed. There *is* a lake right here."

He laughs. "All the ones *I* know do. It's salt water or nothing." When he looks at me, his eyes are bright.

I grin and rub the spot again. It's almost dry. "So, will you see your mother at Thanksgiving?" That's the kind of thing that people ask about missing parents, isn't it?

"Um, probably not." He leans forward to scratch his ankle. "Since she stopped drinking, she's into this nonstop Jesus stuff, which is driving everybody crazy. Especially me. I'm beginning to think she should've stuck to the booze." He rearranges his sock. "What are *you* doing?"

So his mother *drinks.* Or used to. "Mother's cooking dinner," I reply, then lean down to scratch my ankle, too. Why does an itch on one person turn up as an itch on another person? It happens a lot. "Dick and Todd and Serena are coming over."

He clears his throat. Germs are multiplying even as we speak. So far, though, I'm immune. His eyes travel to my face, rest a second, then depart. I wish his eyes would stay longer.

"So where's your dad eating?" he asks, heading south for another ankle scratch.

"He and Janice always go to a restaurant with her sister and husband. None of them likes to cook." Tri comes back up. This time my ankle stays quiet, but I know the itch is still there, waiting.

We sit in silence for a minute.

"Well," I say, at the same exact moment he blurts out, "So—" We look at each other and laugh, and my eyes fill up with warm butterscotch. I can almost taste it on my tongue. Then I can.

We don't channel too long, because he has to stop and use a tissue. Plus we're outside and I'm beginning to feel cold. Still, when he smiles and comes back for a second round, I forget about the temperature, especially when he slips his hand inside my jacket. He just runs it lightly over my shirt, over my right breast, but my nipple wakes up and his thumb finds it. This is pretty nice, but then he jerks away abruptly and explodes in a sneeze.

"Dammit!" He does tissue duty. "Stupid idiot cold."

"That's okay." Is he too sick to continue? He tastes pretty good, despite the germs.

"I'm gonna be sick for sure on Thanksgiving. Even if I get a fever of a hundred and five, though, I'm still going."

"Going?"

He coughs into his fist. "To New Orleans," he says,

looking at me. The afternoon is turning late and cold and his eyes are as dark as the water. "To see my father."

A straggly family moves toward the pier. The mother grips the toddler's hand while the father oversees their other kid. They move out over the water. Nobody falls in.

"He lives in New Orleans?" I watch Tri start to blend into the coming dusk. The straggly family leaves the pier. They didn't stay long.

"Yeah. I found his address on the Internet."

"Oh. You didn't know where he lived?"

Tri shrugs. "He hasn't had anything to do with me since I was two or something. He just took off. Nobody knew where he went—not even his parents." He makes a noise sort of like a strangled snort and coughs. If we're going to channel some more, shouldn't we do it before the phlegm situation worsens?

"I think everyone was happy he left," he continues. "He always screwed everything up, getting in trouble all the time. Nothing big—just *stuff.* Booze, drugs, fighting. Not to mention making *me.*"

My ankle itches again. I reach down to scratch. "So, um, why?"

Tri sniffs and looks at me. "Why what?"

"Why did he leave? Move so far away?" Dad left, but at least he stayed in Maryland.

Tri laughs. "Probably because he owed everybody money."

"Didn't he even say good-bye?"

"Um, I don't remember. I was pretty young." He shrugs. "See, what happened is, he met my mom at this club. They discovered they both liked booze better than anything else, so they partied hard and did the big bang sex thing for a couple of months, then called it off." He laughs. "Romantic, huh? I'm the leftovers."

"Well, he'll be glad to see you," I say, picturing a big white man hugging Tri, crying because he's so happy to see his son.

Tri clears his throat. "He doesn't know I'm coming."

Huh? "You're just going to show up? What if he didn't cook a turkey?"

He laughs and smacks me lightly on top of my head. "That's what I like about you, Robin. You're always thinking." He does that strangled snort-thing again.

Is he making fun of me? I'm ready to get mad, but his hand finds mine, his fingers curling around my palm. He looks at me seriously, and I understand that this is important.

"I'm leaving Thursday night after the turkey gobble, when everyone's asleep. If I drive straight through, just stopping at a rest area for a nap, I should get there sometime Friday night. Then I'll leave Saturday night and get back here on Sunday." He puts our hands in his lap and cups them with his other hand. "The mean aunt doesn't know I'm going."

"Really? My mother would *kill* me!"

"Well, I'm leaving a note. But if I told her my plan ahead of time, she'd never let me go. She hates my father's guts. And she'd never let me drive that far south on my own. She thinks if you're black, you get murdered as soon as you enter Mississippi. But she's stuck in the past. *Tons* of black people live in Mississippi, right? And they're doing okay. Besides, I'll be on the interstate." He coughs. "I'm not stupid. I know what can happen. I deal with it every day of my life."

The light on his hair is turning it a new color. *Toffee.* "What can happen?"

He snorts incredulously. "What can *happen*?" He stares at me, his eyes hot on my face. "What planet do you live on?"

Oh. The stupid white people planet. Despite the chill, flames burn my skin. I study my feet. My shoes are caked with mud.

He stares at the lake. I hesitate, then reach and touch his hair. It's soft and springy.

He runs his hands over his knees. "Aunt Betsy and Uncle Ted want me to be black—period. And I am. That's what I am." He's silent a moment. "My white relatives—the ones who acknowledge me—want me to be an interesting, intelligent mix they can show off to their friends." He laughs. "Tri the social project! But tell me this—" He holds his hand up, turning his sandy palm to face me. "While everybody's figuring out what color I am, why don't they ever say I'm white?" His eyes glint in the dusk. "It's not that I want to be. I *don't.* But . . . why can't I ever be like my father?"

I swallow. All I've ever been is a Maryland Caucasian. But if I know one thing, I know that Tri will never be considered white. "You're butterscotch," I say. "That's just a fact." I already told him so, outside the Moo Palace.

"A fact, huh?" He sniffs and digs for another tissue. He must have an entire box of Kleenex stashed in different parts of his clothing. I wait while he blows his nose; then we sit and stare at the lake until it disappears into the dark.

* * *

Back in his car, Tri punches up that smooth, wraparound music again—some kind of crooning, throbbing love song. I don't know who's singing, and I don't want to interrupt to ask.

We listen all the way home, one song after another, not saying anything until he pulls up in front of my house. Then he turns it off, and the silence is sudden and loud. "Bye, Robin."

He doesn't say anything else. It sounds final, like I'm never going to see him again.

"Bye," I say, undoing my seat belt, feeling myself sink into black, salty water. I don't want to go. I stare out the window. Frankie's Probe is parked next door, so he must be home. Maybe he—

Janice! What if he's with her? I have to—

Tri leans and puts his hand on the back of my neck, pulling my face over. His mouth finds my lips and his other hand opens my jacket and finds my breasts. This is where we left off! His hair is a soft tease against my face. But when I run my hand over his thigh and touch his *thing,* starting to give it a massage, he stops abruptly, pulling back. He removes my hand and rests his forehead against mine, his breath ragged.

"Um, you better go in," he says, "before your posse shows up." I can hear him swallow. "Maybe we need to take this a little bit slower, okay? I mean—" He shrugs. "I just need, I don't know, space or something." He pushes my hair back from my face. "Okay?"

"Okay." No *thing* touching?

He sits back. "Man. I never thought I'd hear myself say *that* to a girl."

Is it because I'm a piggy? A *white* piggy?

The front door opens and Mother sticks her head out. She smiles and waves, then goes back in.

"Posse time," says Tri. He squeezes my hand. "You okay?"

"Yes." No. "Bye."

"Bye."

I get out and walk up the sidewalk. I still don't know if I'm ever going to see him again.

Nineteen

Nineteen

Mother, now wrapped in a blanket on the couch, is blowing her nose, watching the final scenes from *Mary Poppins.* I've never told anyone, but it's my favorite movie in the whole world. Except, I hate it that Mary Poppins goes away at the end. Why can't she stay forever? When I was little, I used to wait for her to come visit *me,* but she never did.

I also really like the penguins.

Mother explodes in a sneeze. "Uh," she says, her voice all snaggled up. "Bring me a Pepsi, would you, sweetie? Over ice. I feel like I'm dying." She honks into her tissue.

I discover Dick in the kitchen, heating up a pot of homemade chicken soup. I see a big plastic container, so he must have made it at his house, then brought it over. "Soup for the sick," he explains, and I see that this is how he takes care of people. He asks me how my date went. I'm not really sure it was a date, especially since Tri's *thing* is off-limits and he maybe doesn't like me.

"It was okay," I answer. I pour Mother's Pepsi, watching it fizz up to the top of the glass, then take it to her. Mary Poppins, umbrella open, feet pointed outward, is starting to rise into the sky—*leaving*. Since I can't stand this part, I go back to the kitchen.

"We skipped stones, except all of mine sank right away." I take a slug of Mother's leftover Pepsi.

Dick nods. "I know what that's like. But it really just comes down to basic science, and practice." He stirs the soup, lifting a spoonful and inhaling. "Nothing like hot soup on a cold night. Here, write this down."

I grab a piece of paper and pencil as he stirs and talks. "A flat stone, plus rate of speed, adding in, of course, the functional weight of water surface, equals the thrust of air pressure over each electrical zone layer, squared." I get it half written down before I realize he's joking. He chucks me under the chin and laughs, handing me a bowl of soup. "I could never skip the darn things either. Here, take this to your mother."

I head for the living room, trying not to spill. Is *this* what it means to have a stepfather?

We eat in front of the TV, slurping and watching *60 Minutes*—something about sneaky bank practices. The show is sixty minutes too long, but Mother thinks she knows something after she watches it.

The soup is thick and tastes a lot better than what you get in a can. It's got big fat noodles in it instead of little skinny ones. When no one's looking, I fish out a chicken chunk and roll it up in a noodle. A little chicken soup sub!

So far, like me, Dick doesn't have any germs. I'm hoping this means he'll be making the Thanksgiving turkey, as Mother's always comes out all dried up. Dick told me how to make cranberry sauce from scratch—boil the cranberries in sugar!—so I'm going to buy a bag of fresh berries at Super Food and cook some.

Fifty minutes is all I can take of *60 Minutes.* Now they're showing devious medical practices. "I'm going next door to water the plants," I announce, standing up. Mrs. Jenkins and her boyfriend are coming down on Tuesday. Mother's dying to see if he's as fat and bald as she thinks he is.

"Okay," she says, sniffing into a tissue. She snuggles against Dick as a hidden camera shows a doctor being sneaky with his prescription pad.

I put on my jacket.

A breeze has picked up, and it's not just chilly now—it's cold. Still, I have a mission. I quietly cross Frankie's yard to the back of his house, scrunching my jacket up higher around my neck. Light floods from the little window above Frankie's room. When I get close, I squat down.

Volleyball!

My heart starts racing, my throat gets tight, and my stomach clenches into a knot. Why can't Frankie find someone to cheat with who isn't married to my father? He and Janice are on his bed. He's wearing his favorite outfit—nothing—and she's got on some little tiny red Victoria's Secret kind of thing. It's pulled off her shoulders so her breasts are exposed—I guess when the rest of her looks like the old Mrs. Muir, she'll still have those big bazooms sticking out. Frankie can't keep his hands or mouth off them.

They lock tongues, and I watch Janice stroke his thing, then lean down and put her mouth on it. I never did that. Was I supposed to?

Snap. What's that?

I spring upward just as someone shrieks and grabs my shoulder. I stumble, landing on my knees, then frantically shove myself upright, my body screaming, *Run*!

China.

I sink quietly back to my haunches, heart stopped.

She crouches before the window, her jacket bunched around her hips, her mouth opened in a silent O, her eyes wide. "No!" she cries, raising her purse. I lunge at her just as she slams it against the glass. *Crack!* Sprawled on the ground, I raise my head far enough to see Frankie and Janice staring at the window, fear and shock streaked across their faces, desperately trying to cover themselves.

"Damn you!" China screams, ramming her purse once more into the window, splintering it further. She pulls herself to her feet, looks at me for one moment—her eyes big horrible dark circles—then turns on her heel and runs.

"China!" I yell, scrambling up, floundering after her, tripping. "China!" I'm finally up, running.

She makes it all the way around the front of the house, almost to her car, where she crashes into Dick.

"Hey!" he says, grabbing her arms. "China! Good heavens—what's wrong?"

I catch up, air squeezed from my lungs, just as she lets out another shriek and crumbles against his chest, sobbing. Dick holds her as Mother, who must have been waving good-bye to him from the front door, comes running down the walk.

"China! Honey! What's wrong?"

"Frankie!" China half sobs, half screams. "Frankie! He's—that bastard! He's with, with—" Her voice strangles in tears.

Mother looks at me, bewildered.

The parallel universe settles like a thick silence over my shoulders. I can hardly breathe.

"Janice," I finally say, my voice raspy. "He's with . . . Janice."

"China!" It's Frankie, wrapped in his short white terry-cloth robe, tearing out the front of his house. "China!" He's running toward us, and I see our neighbor across the street open his front door and step out, releasing a flood of light.

China jerks away from Dick. "You stay away from me, you bastard!" she screams at Frankie. "You go to hell!" She runs to her car and pulls the door open and jumps in. Somewhere, I hear another car pull up, a door opening and shutting. Who else is watching?

Frankie yanks the handle on the passenger side of China's car, but she's got it locked. "China!" he yells. "Open this fucking door!" But she starts the engine and floors it, roaring away, making Frankie jump back.

Her tires squeal down the street, then a moment of silence ensues. The neighbor across the way keeps watching. Frankie stands stupidly in his bare feet, staring at the sidewalk, running his fingers through his hair over and over again, his legs naked under the bottom of his robe. Dick is silent. Mother, staring at Frankie, stands with her hand clasped over her mouth.

A little *click tap click* sounds—high heels. Janice, fully dressed, strides down Frankie's front walk toward her car, her coat over her arm, not even looking at us. She gets in her black Celica, starts the engine, and takes off.

Footsteps approach from the other direction, quiet but steady, and we turn to look.

Dad.

"You bastard," he growls, staring at Frankie. Frankie looks frantically from Dad to Mother to me. He starts to back away.

"Hey, man—"

"You stinking son of a bitch!" Dad shouts. He lunges for Frankie, but Frankie turns and runs toward his house. Stumbling once, he disappears inside the front door.

"That fucking bastard," Dad shrieks—but his voice breaks. He tries to muffle his sobs with his hands, but I can still hear them. Mother touches his arm. Dick, his mouth twisted, his hands knotted into fists, says, "I'm sorry, Brad. I'm really sorry." He turns and walks toward our front door. Mother motions with her head for me to follow, and I do. When I look back, Mother has her arms around Dad.

I've never seen that before.

Dick sets a mug of instant hot chocolate with extra marshmallows in front of me on the kitchen table. I sip and almost burn my tongue, but I still can't stop shaking. Dick slides his chair real close and puts his arm around me. "I'm sorry, honey. What a night." He hands me a napkin and I blot my face. My stomach is squeezed so tight it hurts. He pulls me close and I bury myself in his chest, but I can't relax. I feel like I'm about to break apart.

I hear the front door open and shut. Mother comes

into the kitchen and touches me on the shoulder, leaving her hand there for a moment, then sits down. I separate from Dick's chest, and he gets up to pour Mother a mug of chocolate. Mostly she just holds it. Her face is tired, her eyes puffy, her hair every which way.

"I can't believe it," she says. "That Frankie would do such a thing." Her voice is low, hoarse now from her cold. "I've known that boy for years. Sure, he likes his fun—good grief, we all like to flirt—but *this*!" She takes a sip of chocolate. "He's crazy about China; I know he is. *Crazy*. How could he do this? And—as much as I hate to say it—with a member of *my* family?"

Tears flood her eyes, and she blots them with a ragged tissue. "Now, Janice—her I believe. From the moment I met her, I knew just what kind of person she was. Your father was a fool to—" She looks at me and stops. "Well." She taps her Dark Lilac Rhapsody fingernails against her mug and sighs deeply. "What a mess."

Nobody says anything. The parallel universe is quiet.

She runs her fingers through her hair. "I know how much you looked up to Frankie," she says, studying my face. "I know this has to hurt." Sniffing, she blots her nose with her mangled tissue. "What a disappointment." She clears her throat and stares at the table. "What a disaster."

"How did Brad find out?" Dick reaches for the box of tissues on the counter and hands it to Mother. She takes a fresh one.

"He came home from his trip a day early. When he got in this evening, he found a message from Frankie on their answering machine." She shakes her head. "He's shattered. Just shattered." She looks at Dick. "I would never do that to you. You know that, don't you?"

Dick reaches to curl his fingers around hers. "I know. And I would never do that to you." They smile quietly at each other, and I see that they *do* know.

I gulp my chocolate down and go upstairs. My room is cold. I pull on my flannel nightgown, then climb into bed, pulling the blankets up around my chin, waiting for the sheets to get warm. Maybe everything will be all right. Maybe Dad and Janice will make up. Maybe China and Frankie will get back together. It happens all the time in *People* magazine. Movie stars always cheat on their girlfriends and wives, and—okay—usually they dump them for new girlfriends and wives, but sometimes they don't. Sometimes they stay together.

Feeling better, I let my eyes shut. Maybe Mary Poppins is headed for my house *right now*. It's not too late! I'm not *that* old. Maybe the penguins are coming!

Dad looks something like a penguin—he's shaped like a pear.

My eyes feel full of grit. I never thought I'd see him cry.

3:36 A.M.

The darkness of the room opens in my eyes.

What if China had seen *me*?

The house is quiet. I get out of bed and tiptoe down the hall, feeling my way in the dark. I peek out the end window. Frankie's house is pitch-black. Is he asleep, his *thing* small and sad between his legs? Is it dreaming of *something beautiful*? Is it dreaming of China?

I tiptoe quietly back to bed, leaving the cold air of my room for the warmth still trapped between my sheets.

I squeeze my eyes shut, but I still picture China's face,

the way it looked tonight—crying, crushed, and broken. And Dad's. I want his face to go away, but it doesn't.

Now I know what someone looks like when they've just encountered the parallel universe.

I don't ever want to see that face again.

Twenty

Twenty

Mother's cold is better. She sounds worse but says she feels better. In her pink quilted robe and the pink rabbit slippers she hardly ever wears, she keeps peering out the living room blinds, checking to see if Mrs. Jenkins is home yet. Today's the big day—Tuesday—when the ugly boyfriend is supposed to appear. It's almost ten P.M., though, and the only car in Frankie's driveway is his.

I follow Mother into the kitchen. When I finished my bath and came down and saw that she was wearing her rabbit slippers, I ran back upstairs and got mine. Mine are blue, like my robe. I pointed them out to Mother and she smiled. They were a Christmas gift last year from Serena. Our feet are the only things about us that come close to matching.

Neither of us has seen or talked to Frankie since Sunday. I haven't even checked on the plants.

"What if he's drinking again, or doing drugs?" she

blurts out, standing beside the phone. She sounds like a frog with a megaphone. I guess the drug angle gives her enough incentive, because she finally stops tapping her nails on the kitchen counter and dials.

"Frankie, hi! It's Claire. . . . Yes, it's me! I've got that cold going around. So how are you? . . . I see. Well, I'm not surprised. But you're not doing anything, are you? I mean, drinking, or . . . Good. Good. . . . I was worried."

Mother shifts her weight from one pink rabbit to the other. "Well, look, is your mother coming home for the holiday? . . . She's not. I see. . . . Well, the neighbors are talking, of course, but that's what neighbors—yes, I know. . . . Well, you can't stay inside forever. . . . What? That's crazy! You only missed one night! And a Monday! Nobody drinks on Monday. Lots of places aren't even *open* on Monday! Call Raze and tell them . . . They won't, huh. . . . Well, you're right, there's plenty of . . . yes . . . absolutely. You won't have any trouble finding a . . . Good idea. Try there."

She sniffs loudly and clears her throat, and I slide the tissue box down the counter. She pulls out a fresh one and holds it against her nose. "Well, I can't stand to think of you alone on Thanksgiving. You can always come over here. . . . No, of course I wouldn't invite you if Brad was coming. . . . Well, he has to deal with it, and so does Janice, and so do . . . Yes, I know, you made a terrible mistake, but Janice was in on it, too, she was half of it. . . . Yes, well, that's just the way it is. . . . Now listen, honey, we love you. . . . I'll call. . . . Okay. Bye."

She hangs up and blows her nose. "I knew his mother wouldn't show." She throws her tissue into the trash and pulls another one out of the box. "She nabs this fancy *executive*, so at the first hint of trouble, she runs—like she's too good for this neighborhood now. Some mother *she's* turned out to be! No wonder Frankie's messed up!"

She washes her hands and pulls tomorrow's lunch material out of the refrigerator. Low-fat turkey. Doesn't she know I'll be eating a whole bunch of regular-fat turkey in two days?

"Well, I went ahead and invited him for Thanksgiving, but he said no. He's too embarrassed. I understand that. I feel conflicted myself. But I can't just walk away from him. He's a good kid; he is! He just needs direction." She lays open two slices of skinny low-calorie bread on the counter. "Don't misunderstand. I feel terrible about your father. I do. I mean, we've had our differences, but I hate to see him torn up this way. It hurts me, truly. But what can I do? He keeps running after these bimbos!"

She rips a leaf of iceberg lettuce off and rinses it under the faucet. That's the vegetable part of my lunch. The low-cal mayonnaise is the fat part. The fruit is the apple she's about to wash.

The piggy part will be the Twinkie.

No school till Monday! Some stupid early news show is on TV. Hasn't anyone figured out yet that news is boring?

Traffic report: shots of cars backed up forever on the Beltway, in the holiday rush to get out of town. It's *crowded*. Big *duh*.

Weather report: fair skies ahead for Dead Turkey Day. Snore.

* * *

I jerk awake as Mother's key turns the lock in the front door. My dream shreds—an image of Frankie's geranium, its pale pink flowers falling like snow, alone and naked in the window of his old bedroom.

I pull myself upright as Mother pushes the door open, exasperated. "I've got four more bags of groceries in the car!" she exclaims, landing a bag on the floor with a thump. "I could use some help!" As I get up, a woman on the TV screen is smiling, showing me her long, beautiful golden hair. "Hair that you dare!" she says, laughing and caressing a bottle of Shine-S-ence conditioner. "Hair that makes him care!"

China's hair is thick and honey-blond and wavy. It always smells like flowers.

Mother and I carry in the rest of Thanksgiving dinner. She bought a fresh turkey and is planning to cook it herself. There's still time, though, for Dick to intervene.

After dinner, after the stores have closed, just as Mother's getting ready to chop walnuts for her special cottage cheese–lime Jell-O salad, we get an emergency call from Serena about missing ingredients. She's making her special cheese-stuffed mushrooms. We ransack the cupboards and Mother finds a can of bread crumbs. She dashes out the door to rush them over.

I wait a minute, then grab my box of smoky blue stationery and do my own dash. I figure I've got about an hour before she finishes yakking and gets back.

* * *

I knock on Tri's front door. It took me twelve minutes to get here. I practically ran.

The door opens. The mean aunt stares at me. She's wearing jeans and a sweatshirt, and her hair's braided in a whole bunch of little braids and pulled up into a spiraled do. Does she remember me?

"Um, hi, Mrs. Beech. Is, uh, Tri home?"

The Becky brat sticks her head around the door. "It's Robin *bir-r-r-d*!" she shrieks. Shouldn't they consider a muzzle? Her hair's smoothed out and rolled under, like she's going to church or something. She's got a little pink barrette in it.

The mean aunt's eyes impale me for a minute; then she steps back. "Hello, Robin. Come in. Tri just got home." She looks at the Beck-womp. "Tell Tri he's got company."

Becky prances off. "Tri!" I hear her screech. "It's Robin *bir-r-rd*!"

I step into the hall and smile at the mean aunt. She gives me a tight smile back. "It's getting late," she comments. "You walk here alone?" She obviously doesn't approve.

"Um, yes," I reply. "But it's okay, because I'm on a special mission." She stares at me. "Concerning mermaids," I add.

The mean aunt lifts her eyebrows. "Mermaids?" She narrows her eyes and studies me like I'm an abstract modern sculpture. "I think I'll just leave that one alone," she says. Mother would agree with her lipstick choice—a dark bloodred.

Ray skids into the hallway, stopping abruptly when he sees me. "Hi!" he says. "I got a new game!" He waves a hand computer game thing. It probably laser-zaps innocent teenage girls on sight. "Wanna see it?"

"Um, sure."

He starts toward me, but Becky reappears. "He says to come into the dining room. He's *eating*." She states this as if he's busy working on a new ship design for trans-world space travel and shouldn't be interrupted.

Aunt Betsy nods and Becky and Ray guide me through the living room. It doesn't look especially *black*. It looks a lot like it did when Melissa lived here—rumpled up with junk and magazines and books, the furniture covered with throws. The serious uncle looks up from the TV—he's watching a *Bust!* rerun—and pauses his eyes on me, then smiles absently and waves me forward with the remote. I'm sure I feel the mean aunt's eyes drilling into my back as Ray's computer game bings and beeps and zings. We enter the dining room, where my escorts announce, in unison, "She's here!"

Tri, wearing an open blue flannel shirt over a white tee, is busy sticking a hunk of sausage into his mouth. His hair is still a floppy moppy butterscotch bush. He spears a hunk of scrambled egg on his fork and waves it at me, then points to the chair across from his. I sit down, putting my stationery box on the table. Schoolbooks and papers are piled next to me, along with folded towels and a pair of jeans. Ray leans against my chair, working his game. Becky rests on Tri's arm. He immediately shrugs her off.

"I'm eating, Beck! Give me some room." His voice has gone down about two octaves with his cold.

She sniffs. "Mama says since you're sick, you should be having *soup*."

"I'm eating what I'm eating, okay?" He smiles at me. "So how ya doing?"

I smile back a little. "Okay. I—"

"Got it!" Ray shrieks in my ear, making me jump. He waves the game at Tri, grinning. A whole bunch of little buzzy bings sound. At least I didn't get zapped.

"What's up?" Tri asks, swallowing a slug of what looks like hot tea with milk.

"I need to ask you a favor." I look at Becky. "In *private*."

Her eyebrows go up and she turns and leans in front of Tri's face. He sighs loudly. "Becky—disappear, okay? I don't need you in my scrambled eggs. Ray-gun, you too."

Becky sniffs. "Mama won't like you doing *private* stuff in here."

"Take this." Tri hands her his last slice of jellied toast. "Go forth and eat."

She snatches the toast and turns and abruptly marches away. "I'm telling Mama."

Tri glares at Ray until he reluctantly trails Becky out of the room. He waves good-bye as the door swings shut behind him.

Tri coughs and takes another drink of tea.

I fiddle with my box, then clear my throat. "I only have a minute. I have to get home before my mother does." He sniffs and digs out a tissue. I open my box and pull out a skinny wrinkled road map and slide it across the table. "Mobile, Alabama, is only an inch away from New Orleans. It's practically right next door."

He fingers the map, watching me. "And?"

My throat feels scratchy. "I've got an emergency letter that needs to be delivered. To Melissa. In Mobile. Since you're going right there, I thought—"

He clears his throat. "An inch?"

"Yes. It's right on the way. It would only take you a

minute. Here's her street number." I hand him the envelope I've already addressed. "It's easy to find." I hope.

He blots his nose with a tissue. "Why don't you just mail it?"

"Because—" Because of this dream I had last night. I was lying on a beach. It was night, everything was dark and cold. I couldn't move. I thought there was no sound, not even waves, but then I heard something strange and eerie—a mermaid, clinging to rocks, crying. She was so sad, I woke up.

I don't say that, though.

"Because it's *personal.* And I don't want it to get lost. And—" I feel a funny tickle in the back of my throat. Am I getting sick? "Mermaids are involved."

A smile flickers across his face. I wish he still wanted to channel with me.

"Oh. *Mermaids.* Why didn't you just say so?" He fingers the envelope, his eyes warm. "I assume it's stamped First Class Mermaid, ready to go?"

He understands! "Almost." I pull out the top sheet of smoky blue paper from my box of stationery and, just to myself, read what I wrote earlier, during lunch.

Dear Melissa,

You are fine. Mermaids need to be kissed and hugged, or they get sick. This is just a fact. I'm not surprised the Gracie kiss happened in Mobilemess, as you are so close to the greeny gulf. If she kisses you again, and you don't like it, just smack her with your mermy tail. If you do like it, well, it's been established that that kind of thing happens to some people, especially movie stars—it gets written up in People *magazine all the time. Whatever you do, please do not cry alone at night on an empty beach.*

Well, that's all for now. While you were gone, I visited the parallel universe of liars. Also, Dad and Janice might be breaking up.

Yours, sweet tweet Robin

P.S. When you get home at Christmas, I will kiss and hug you, too, but just as a friend.

A tingly rawness scratches at the back of my throat. Ignoring it, I pick up my purple Lizard pen and add one last line.

P.P.S. This is being delivered by Tri. I'm not really sure if he likes me, but he's very nice. Please do not say anything about what color he should be.

Tri gives me a ride home, my sealed letter tucked in his shirt pocket. When we stop in front of my house, I undo my seat belt and he sneezes at the same time as I cough.

"Ugh," he says. "Germs." He blows his nose, then checks his face in the rearview mirror. "I am now a certified snot-free zone."

I giggle and we look at each other. "Be careful," I say. "Driving, I mean. Not just because of my letter. But"—my throat gets thick—"because of, you know, the stuff that can happen."

"Me big strong man," he croaks, thumping his chest. "Oogie-boogies no get *me*!" He grins and I smile crookedly. His hand reaches and curls around mine.

"Bye, Robin."

"Bye." I feel stupid tears in my eyes. What if the

things that can happen, *do* happen? Or what if he likes the greeny gulf so much he doesn't come back? I hold on tight to his hand.

He kisses me on the cheek. His lips are chapped. I kiss him on *his* cheek, and our lips touch, briefly. He smells like someone who's sick, but also like sausage. And Tri. He smells like *Tri.*

"Don't cry, Robin." His tongue touches my face. He's licking a tear! "Me need salt," he continues, growling. He licks another tear, and I start giggling.

He grabs my head and licks me straight across my face from one cheek to the other, over my nose, and I burst out laughing. For a minute we hug, giggling and close, and it feels so delicious I think maybe we'll stay like this forever, but we don't.

"Bye," he says. In the dim light, his eyes gleam. "If the mean aunt doesn't totally kill me, I'll see you when I get back. Okay?"

"Okay." I get out of his car. When I put my key in the front door and turn to wave, he drives off. I listen till I don't hear his car.

When Mother comes in ten minutes later, Flower's blaring, I'm sucking a cherry cough drop and drinking a Diet Pepsi, and a pot of fresh cranberries is working its way to a boil.

"Hmm," Mother says. She likes the jellied cranberry sauce and has two cans in the cupboard for tomorrow. She gets out the cutting board, pops open a Diet Pepsi, and starts chopping walnuts for her special salad.

Tri said he's coming back!

Twenty-one

Everybody but me loves Serena's cheese-stuffed mushrooms. They're huge! I take a bite of one, then hide the rest of it in a napkin. On my next trip to the kitchen, to get Serena a 7UP, I dump it into the trash. Fortunately, since they're being served before dinner, and everyone's still running around and yakking, I don't have to not like it at the table, in front of her.

She's upset about Dad—since Sunday night, she's the only one of us he's talked to, and that's because she called *him.* Mother thinks he's embarrassed and hurt that the Other Man is his ex-wife's neighbor. She says it's a matter of male pride.

You'd think he'd want to talk to *me,* though. Is it my fault that I'm his ex-wife's daughter?

Talking about the *affair* is the only time I've ever heard Serena use bad words. She's furious at Janice and Frankie and periodically looks out the window toward Frankie's house. It's a good thing he's not coming for dinner.

Janice moved out. Dad has already seen a lawyer. He's having Thanksgiving dinner with some friends. Mother just nods her head sympathetically at Serena's periodic outbursts but doesn't say much.

Todd doesn't say much, either. I think he just wants to concentrate on being Serena's husband and his baby's father. He seems happy, as if he's never been a piece of wood. He even jokes around with Dick—I think he actually likes him now. Maybe after the baby's born, he'll even like *me.*

I set the butter dish on the dining room table. I've already put out my homemade cranberry sauce—it tastes yummy!—and filled the water glasses.

There're five of us, but there would still be room for another person. Frankie's car hasn't moved from his driveway all week. He must be down to bread and water by now. And the plants—I try not to think about the plants.

"Dinner!" Dick announces, carrying in a big platter of turkey. He got here early enough to intervene, and the turkey looks and smells terrific. I stirred the gravy while he whipped the potatoes and Mother spooned Cheez Whiz over the brussels sprouts.

Everyone crowds in and sits down. When Mother makes us go around and say what we're grateful for, Todd actually answers. He says he's thankful to have a wonderful wife and a baby on the way. He even reaches for and squeezes Serena's hand in front of everybody. In the spirit of things, I mention I'm happy to be eating turkey again. I also put in a plug for my homemade cranberry sauce.

I keep quiet, though, about Frankie's *thing,* Melissa's

mermy tail, and Tri's butterscotch skin. I don't say anything about *something beautiful.*

"I'm going to water the plants," I announce loudly after dinner. Everyone ignores me. Except for Mother, who's in the kitchen, they're busy watching *The Sound of Music.* The nuns are singing about a problem like Maria. She is a problem. She can't fly, she never dances with the chimney sweeps, and there's no penguins.

I join Mother in the kitchen just as she adds a big spoonful of my homemade cranberry sauce to Frankie's plate.

We survey the mountain of food—slabs of meat, light and dark, a pile of dressing, a boatload of sweet potatoes with marshmallows, a wedge of cottage cheese–lime Jell-O with walnuts, mashed potatoes with gravy, a bucket of brussels sprouts saturated with Cheez Whiz, plus creamed corn and two buttered rolls. And the cranberry sauce. After this, Frankie's belly will be the size of Alaska.

Mother wraps two big sheets of aluminum foil over the whole thing and hands it to me, balancing a smaller foil-wrapped plate of pumpkin pie on top.

I head out into the night.

Juggling the plates, I put the key into Frankie's front door. The house is dark, quiet. I clear my throat. That funny little scratch is worse, and my nose feels prickly. "Frankie?" No response. Do I hear the plants rustling?

Flipping on a light, I go into the kitchen and set the

plates on the counter. The trash can is full of frozen food wrappers, including an ice cream carton. When's the last time I had a Nutsie Boy cone?

I try again. "Frankie?" Silence. He must be asleep.

I slip off my jacket and turn on the water, picking up the little plastic watering can. I snap on the light in each room as I water. Everyone's glad to see me. The African violets in the living room are parched. The snake plants are practically hissing. The maidenhair ferns are pale and close to passing out. Even the cacti want a sip.

When I pass the dollhouse, I gasp. It's been knocked over onto its side, the contents scattered. I step around tiny pieces of furniture. I accidentally crunch a Tiffany lamp.

Swallowing hard, I turn on the lamp in Frankie's old bedroom. The geranium looks terrible. I touch its spindly arms and it barely rustles. I pour in a jumbo gulp. Is it too late? It drinks it all. Maybe there's still hope.

All that's left is the skinny little plant in Frankie's basement apartment. I wait at the top of the stairs. It's dark all the way down. I grit my teeth; then I smack the light switch and descend to the tiny space that makes up Frankie's living room.

The plant's drooping over the side of its pot. I give it a sip, then another. Maybe a song would help. Maybe something from *Mary Poppins*. I open my mouth—

Creak. I swing around, heart pounding.

Frankie is standing in the doorway to his bedroom, wrapped in a blanket. He looks awful—his hair a mess, his face bloated and unshaven, his eyes bloodshot. I can smell the booze across the room. He must have been reestablishing his supplies on the sly.

"Hey, babe," he says, his voice hoarse. At least he's not swaying or anything. Maybe everything's worn off for now. Despite being temporarily unattractive, he seems okay.

"I brought you a plate of food. It's upstairs. Mother and I fixed it."

He slides his fingers through his hair—he definitely needs a shampoo—and the blanket slips off a bare shoulder. "Thanks."

"Mother wants to know if you've heard from China." So do I.

"No."

"Um. Janice?" I hold my breath.

He lets out half a laugh. "Gone with the wind, babe. Your dad can have her."

"I see." Except—he doesn't want her anymore. And—she doesn't want him. I picture Dad eating leftover pumpkin pie all alone in his kitchen, and even though I never liked Janice and she never liked me, I wish she still liked *him*.

Frankie walks back into his darkened bedroom. I hesitate, then follow. He flicks on a little lamp next to his bed, and shadows walk through the room. The window is boarded up. Empty wine bottles and beer cans are scattered on the floor. He sits on the bed.

I decide not to ask about his missing mother. "Got a job yet?"

He sniffs. Is he catching *the cold*? "I called a buddy who tends bar at Distillations. He's getting me on, part-time. Some guy's leaving, so he thinks I can get more hours later." He clears his throat. "Soon as I get some money together, I'm heading for L.A."

He's leaving? I swallow hard. He's *leaving*?

"I gotta get out of this dump, get things moving. Get where something's going on, you know?" Then he looks at me and smiles bitterly, and though I know he's upset, for a moment I almost feel dizzy. Under the bloat, he's still Mr. Studly. It will take only a few days for him to get back into movie star condition.

"How's your stomach?" I ask, my voice tight.

"Stomach?"

I point to his belly.

"Oh, that." He opens his blanket, and his biscuit is still pretty flat. Mostly, though, I look at his thing. It's quiet, cradled in its nest of dark, silky hairs. He looks at me a moment, his eyes bloodshot, then reaches for my hand. I approach the bed, letting him pull me close, the space between my legs waking up, remembering our massages. I know where he wants my hand to go. Maybe I want it to go there, too.

"I can't," I say, my throat dry, as the parallel universe collapses around me. "I can't do that anymore."

His face stiffens in surprise, but he quickly shrugs it off. "Whatever." He wraps the blanket around his shoulders again and stares at the floor. "I'm tired," he says, running his hands through his greasy hair. "Fucking tired. Everything's crap and I'm sick and fucking tired of it."

"Go to sleep," I say.

He looks at me sharply, eyebrows raised. Then he half laughs and shrugs. "Go to sleep," he mutters, mimicking my voice. He shakes his head. "Yes, Mother," he answers, his voice nasty. "Whatever you say, Moth—" His voice breaks and he turns away. Lying down, he rolls over so his back is toward me and I can't see his face.

Touching his shoulder, I feel a tremble running through his body.

"It's okay, Frankie," I whisper, sitting down. I hesitate a moment, then lie beside him, sliding my arm over his chest, my breasts pressed into his back, touching his tears with my fingers. Gradually, he stops crying, and I feel his body slacken, sinking toward sleep.

I roll away, watching the shadows on the ceiling. Tri won't leave for New Orleans until everyone's asleep. Has he written his note yet to the mean aunt? What will she think when she finds it? Will she cry or yell? And the Beck-womp and Ray-gun and the serious uncle? Will they jump in a car and try to follow?

What will Tri think about, when he's all alone on the road—with no one to keep him company except the voices of brokenhearted black men and lonely women, all of them singing about lost love?

Frankie stirs beside me, turning over. Pulling the blanket up around our shoulders, he slides his arms around me, burying his face in the back of my neck so we're lying together like spoons. His smell—Flute and sweat and booze—envelops me like a skin.

This is the closest I've ever been to him. Closer than touching his penis. Closer than I'll ever be again.

He starts to snore gently, and the rhythm of his chest moving in and out makes my eyes begin to flutter. I finally let them shut altogether. Mother's probably still in the kitchen, putting food away. Is Maria singing *do-re-mi*? How come Mary Poppins didn't marry Bert? He would have danced with her forever.

I watch her plunge into the water like a missile from the sky—headfirst, feet out, umbrella shut. When she surfaces, she isn't Mary Poppins anymore, but Melissa, swimming in the greeny gulf.

I swish the currents with my mermy tail, just as something catches my eye. It's Tri, bobbing upright in the swell. He laughs and waves to me; then, with one splash of his powerful tail, he dives, heading out for open sea. Too far!

I swim after him, surprised at how fast I can travel. The water kisses me all over. Who knew you could touch the entire ocean? It's right here!

Snort.

Frankie's mouth is right against my ear, his breath stale. Was I asleep? I disentangle myself from his arms and sit up. By now, the hills are probably dead with the sound of music. Mother will want to know about China.

I tuck the blanket around Frankie's neck so he won't get cold, then head upstairs.

Turning off all the lights as I walk through the house, I stop in the kitchen to put the plates in the refrigerator. Frankie will find them when he wakes up. Finally, I pull on my jacket and step out into the night air.

Just before I close the front door, I hear the tiny voices of grateful plants, singing.

The PARALLEL UNIVERSE of LIARS

Kathleen Jeffrie JOHNSON

A READERS GUIDE

"A vivid character whose innocence, entangled with her yearnings, seems as true as her first-person narrative."
—*Booklist*

QUESTIONS FOR DISCUSSION

1. Robin is certainly unlike teen heroines in many other books and movies. What is your overall impression of her? Would you want to be friends with her? In what ways do you identify with her? The author chose to tell this story through Robin's eyes—why do you think she made this choice?

2. When a writer chooses to narrate a book in the first person, it limits what we know about characters other than the narrator. Do you trust Robin's descriptions and analyses? Do you wish you could get inside the head of any of the other characters—to hear his or her thoughts and feelings? What might Frankie, or Robin's mother, be thinking that Robin doesn't know?

3. Robin encounters and observes a good deal of sex and sexual tension in the story. In the end, what do you think she learns about sex and its connection to relationships? Did the book change your ideas or attitudes about sex and sexuality?

4. "*That's sick. Don't say it again. Don't even think it*" (p. 170).
   Robin must confront a confusing world of unspoken rules, especially when it comes to sex. With regard to sex and desire, how do you decide what is right or wrong, "sick" or normal? In your own life, have you ever been confused about such issues? What are your reactions to the thoughts and behavior of Robin? Of Frankie?

5. What would you say to adults who object to this kind of sexual content in a book for teenagers? Why do you think they would object, and do you agree or disagree with the reasons they might give? If you think the sex scenes are important, why? How would the book be different without them?

QUESTIONS FOR DISCUSSION

6. *I hear a car pull up and Dick comes in. He kisses my mother on the lips, and I see that this is a different kind of kiss. An* I'm yours *kiss* (p. 54).
   Robin is an acute observer, especially of her own family. How do her critical observations affect her relationship with her mother (and with Janice, her father, and Frankie)? Does it make her closer to them, or more distant from them? Do you ever think about your family or friends in an objective way—about the kind of people they are outside your relationship with them?

7. Why is it so difficult for Robin to write a satisfactory letter to Melissa? What does it say about her life that she can't seem to put her experience into words?

8. Robin and Tri's relationship develops slowly. What personal issues (what some people call baggage) do each of them bring to the situation? How are those issues worked out as Robin and Tri become closer? Have you ever been in a relationship (romantic or otherwise) in which you had a problem that seemed to exist outside the relationship but that had a big impact on it?

9. *"What do you mean, I'm not really black?"*
   "You're not. You're butterscotch!"
   . . . *"Well, excuse me, but I'm* plenty *black"* (p. 155).
   Talking about race, or someone's racial identity, can be difficult. What is at the root of Robin and Tri's misunderstanding? Why is race such a sensitive topic? Have you ever been offended in a conversation about race, or have you ever offended someone else, even if you didn't mean to?

10. Have you ever gotten stuck in the parallel universe of liars?

In her own words—
a conversation with

KATHLEEN JEFFRIE JOHNSON

Q. Readers—and aspiring writers—are often curious about how an author starts writing a story. How did you develop your ideas for *Parallel Universe*? How did you come up with such an intriguing cast of characters? Did anything specific inspire or motivate you to write this book?

A. I walk into a story with a notion—an impulse, really—of what I want to write, rather than a whole plot. I usually have a sense of who my main character is, and sometimes know what he or she looks like. With *Parallel Universe,* I had Robin and Frankie pretty much in place from the start. I had to struggle to find Robin's mother. Tri, on the other hand, was a happy surprise. Most characters, thankfully, have a way of showing up just when you need them. As for motivation, I wrote *Parallel Universe* when I was working through thoughts and feelings about sexuality for both teens and adults—the fun and danger associated with sex, the right and wrong of it, the happiness and fears—you know, the easy stuff! I didn't decide to write a book dealing with sex—rather, the book let me know I was asking myself lots of questions about sex.

Q. Many adults (parents, teachers, librarians, etc.) worry about the sexual content of books and other media for teens. How would you respond to adults who object to the sexual content of *Parallel Universe*?

A. I understand that some adults (and teens, too) are unhappy about the sexual content of *Parallel Universe.* I'm not offended that they don't like it: If you write something provocative, you can't be alarmed when people are provoked! Sex, I believe, is the social currency of our time: Just look at almost any movie, TV show, video game, magazine—the big question being asked, I think, is "Are you good at sex?" This question is asked of adults, older teens, and young teens. The answer somehow defines our worth. I think many adults are alarmed because they sense that this is an unfair question, for everyone, but especially for young teens. (When I was growing up, in the 1950s and early '60s, the question seemed to be "So, how's the weather?" The total avoidance of sex as a real topic was unfair, too.) Am I asking the "Are you good at sex?" question in *Parallel Universe*, by showing fairly graphic sexual activity? I'm not sure. I try to take Robin and Tri beyond that, to a place where they can find out on their own just who they are.

Q. Related to the above question, some of the sexual aspects of this book are less "mainstream" than those found in other young adult novels. For example, Robin watching through a window as her neighbor has sex, sexual activity between a teenager and a man in his twenties, and blatant infidelity. Why did you go outside the standard norms in this book?

A. I like the scene where Robin is peering through the window watching Frankie and China having sex, while they in turn are lifting their heads to watch porn on video. I think people do that a lot. Not necessarily literally, but in the sense that we tend to look at what others are doing, not just for the excitement of being a voyeur, the dangerous thrill of transgression, but also for affirmation, maybe to see if we're any good ourselves, if we can compare. (And also, perhaps, because watching is sometimes easier than doing.) Robin is learning about sex. Not just the mechanics involved, but the social proprieties attached. A big part of our culture says *Look! Do!* She has to decide on her own what her boundaries will be, and whether she's willing to respect the boundaries of others. As for Robin having a relationship with a man in his early twenties, well, that sometimes happens. No point in pretending it doesn't. Part of Robin's struggle is to see the dangers involved and to extricate herself. Face it, sometimes no one is around to help.

Q. Robin is not your typical teen fiction heroine. By usual standards, she isn't "cute," plucky, likable, or admirable. How did you go about creating the character of Robin? As a literary technique, what were your thoughts when making Robin the narrator, the link between the reader and the entire story?

A. I don't think I had a literary technique when I wrote *Parallel Universe.* Robin was just there, and so was her voice. She may not be typically cute, typically likable, but really, how many people are? A lot of us, both teenagers and adults, are mostly just ordinary, having our own particular good points and pleasantries and smarts, but also our own private brands of surliness and temper, not to mention many, many bad hair days. Books are often written about the attention-getters—the gorgeous, the tragic, the overachievers, the act-out-all-over extroverts—and that's fun, why not? But my interest tends to lie with the grumpy among us. We're people, too.

Q. What do you like—and dislike—about writing in the first person? How did you get into Robin's "head" in order to write this story in her voice?

A. Robin's voice was already in my head, so I didn't have to get into hers. We coexisted for a while in the same body, sort of like commingled space aliens. What I like about writing in the first person is the immediacy of being smack in the middle of your character's life. Her eyes are your eyes, you see what she sees. There's no boundary to cross. What I don't like about first person is the converse—you're stuck in your character's head. The only way to find out what Tri's thinking, for example, is to describe his actions, relay his words—all filtered through Robin's perceptions. I have to hope that this is enough to allow the reader to see and understand Tri.

Q. Robin is always watching people—their expressions, the looks they exchange, etc.—to read their thoughts and intentions. Is this something you do yourself? Do you tend to analyze people in real life, to speculate about their thoughts and try to explain their behaviors? Does this help you as a writer?

A. Yes, yes, and yes. I am a hopeless introvert. It takes lots of caffeine for me to become lively and outgoing, and then I get jittery and miserable and usually regret everything I've said while under the influence. Observing people to figure out their personalities, their motives, their next moves, is a survival technique for the shy. It saves lots of spoken words. And it helps me as a writer, because having spent so much time in other people's heads, it's easy for me to create characters and step inside their skin. The downside is, there's more to life than just sitting on your fanny observing others. Some people actually get up and walk around and do things. I'm still working on that one.

Q. In the end, Robin handles everything pretty well. Things are okay with her mom, Tri offers the promise of something real, she accepts and supports Melissa, and she still feels tender toward Frankie. Did you consider other endings? What would your advice be

to teens who are perhaps facing similar situations in real life?

A. Actually, my original notion for *Parallel Universe* was that it would be a tragedy of sorts. I even had Robin pregnant at one time. Then I thought—*Nah.* I couldn't bear the thought of writing such a sad story. I wanted things to end well for Robin, I wanted her to stumble, then discover she had the inner strength that would allow her to step away from Frankie. I'm not sure how exceptional she is in that. Yes, Robin is potentially in danger, as are many teenagers in real life. I think, though, that while some kids fall all the way down the well, many ultimately reach the right conclusions about the choices they need to make, and pull themselves back up—it just might take a while. As for giving a teenager advice, I can't, really, other than: Use your head, not just your heart and your body. While most people are trustworthy, many will use you simply to satisfy their own needs. When it comes to sex, adults can be greedy; they don't necessarily have your best interests at heart.

Q. Racial issues can be difficult to talk about. As Robin and Tri demonstrate, sometimes even with the best intentions you can say something offensive, or be unsure as to what another's racial identity means to him or her. What do you think about the state of race relations in our country today?

A. Racial issues are indeed a minefield. I basically have two impulses: run like hell in the other direction before everything blows up, or skip merrily across the field, picking daisies. I seem to do both at different times. Race relations today, from my point of view, are both static (things will never change) and in constant, fluid motion (everything's changing!). The contradiction gives a lively, bubbling energy to our lives, which can be exhilarating, exhausting, exasperating. I think most people—both white and black—have some tension regarding race. Maybe a little, maybe a lot. There's no point in not recognizing that. Writing about it can be tricky, though. Filled with good intentions, you want to treat your characters with an openness of heart and a generosity of spirit—and in a way that won't make anybody mad at you! It's my belief, though, that most of us, of whatever shade or color, aren't saints when it comes to race. It's important to be honest with yourself.

Q. This is your first published book—a very remarkable debut. What is your history as a writer? Do you have plans for more books? Any advice to aspiring writers?

A. I spent years and years writing poetry—my first love—then many years writing short stories, then a couple of years writing very bad novels. Let's just say it took me a while to find my fiction voice. I have another young adult novel, *Target*, published in the fall of 2003, and a third book is in the works. I hope to write forever, but I'm not sure that's something I can arrange. The topics that interest me are, I think, the same ones that interest most people, including teens: birth and death, and everything that happens in between, and—that most important question of all—why are we here? As far as the process of producing a book is concerned, the happiest part is the writing itself; the most difficult, being exposed. (Sometimes introverts just don't have any fun.) My tip for aspiring writers, besides *Read, read, read*, is—write! Nothing else will substitute. You either need to do it or you don't. But give yourself and your words time to grow.

Q. Have you ever gotten stuck in the parallel universe of liars? Any tips to readers who are trying to avoid it?

A. *Ahem.* So, how's the weather? Parallel universe, me? Well, I've never been in the exact situation Robin is in, but I think most of us enter a parallel universe of one sort or another from time to time. We all find ourselves contemplating or even trying out a different experience or an alternate life. There's nothing wrong with the fantasy; in real life, however, real people can sometimes get hurt. Maybe it's you, maybe it's someone else. There might be consequences you won't see or understand till later, when it's too late to fix anything or apologize—or punch someone in the nose! Regrets are no fun.

RELATED TITLES

A Dance for Three

Louise Plummer

0-440-22714-3

When she finds out she's pregnant at age fifteen, Hannah Ziebarth believes she will be all right. She will start a family with Milo, and the three of them will live happily ever after. Then reality hits hard.

Shadow People

Joyce McDonald

0-440-22807-7

Four totally different teenagers are thrown together by accident. Or maybe they were destined to meet, for they share emotions that unite them—loneliness, frustration, and anger. Together, in the dark of night, they are drawn to violence like moths to a flame.

Crooked

Laura and Tom McNeal

0-440-22946-4

Clara never thought life could be so intense in the ninth grade—where thrills, heartbreak, and intimidation can take place at a locker, in the lunchroom, or in a bathroom stall.

Her Father's Daughter

Mollie Poupeney

0-440-22879-4

As she grows up in the 1930s in Oregon logging country, Maggie buys her first bra, discovers that a best friend can also be a boyfriend, and struggles with the leering advances of older men. In this world, the only constant is her ever-emerging sense of self.

Counting Stars

David Almond

0-440-41826-7

With stories that shimmer and vibrate in the bright heat of memory, David Almond creates a glowing mosaic of his life growing up in a large, loving Catholic family in northeastern England.

Heaven Eyes

David Almond

0-440-22910-3

Erin Law and her friends in the orphanage are labeled Damaged Children. They run away one night, traveling downriver on a raft. What they find on their journey is stranger than you can imagine.

Kit's Wilderness

David Almond

0-440-41605-1

Kit Watson and John Askew look for the childhood ghosts of their long-gone ancestors in the mines of Stoneygate.

Skellig

David Almond

0-440-22908-1

Michael feels helpless because of his baby sister's illness, until he meets a creature called Skellig.

Before We Were Free

Julia Alvarez

0-440-23784-X

Under a dictatorship in the Dominican Republic in 1960, young Anita lives through a fight for freedom that changes her world forever.

Becoming Mary Mehan: Two Novels

Jennifer Armstrong

0-440-22961-8

Set against the events of the American Civil War, *The Dreams of Mairhe Mehan* depicts an Irish immigrant girl and her family, struggling to find their place in the war-torn country. *Mary Mehan Awake* takes up Mary's story after the war, when she must begin a journey of renewal.

Forgotten Fire

Adam Bagdasarian

0-440-22917-0

In 1915, Vahan Kenderian is living a life of privilege when his world is shattered by the Turkish-Armenian war.

The Rag and Bone Shop

Robert Cormier

0-440-22971-5

A seven-year-old girl is brutally murdered. A twelve-year-old boy named Jason was the last person to see her alive—except, of course, for the killer. Unless *Jason* is the killer.

Dr. Franklin's Island

Ann Halam

0-440-23781-5

A plane crash leaves Semi, Miranda, and Arnie stranded on a tropical island, totally alone. Or so they think. Dr. Franklin is a mad scientist who has set up his laboratory on the island, and the three teens are perfect subjects for his frightening experiments in genetic engineering.

When Zachary Beaver Came to Town

Kimberly Willis Holt

0-440-23841-2

Toby's small, sleepy Texas town is about to get a jolt with the arrival of Zachary Beaver, billed as the fattest boy in the world. Toby is in for a summer unlike any other—a summer sure to change his life.

The Parallel Universe of Liars

Kathleen Jeffrie Johnson

0-440-23852-8

Surrounded by superficiality, infidelity, and lies, Robin, a self-described chunk, isn't sure what to make of her hunky neighbor's sexual advances, or of the attention paid by a new boy in town who seems to notice more than her body.

Ghost Boy

Iain Lawrence

0-440-41668-X

Fourteen-year-old Harold Kline is an albino—an outcast. When the circus comes to town, Harold runs off to join it in hopes of discovering who he is and what he wants in life. Is he a circus freak or just a normal guy?

Lord of the Nutcracker Men

Iain Lawrence

0-440-41812-7

In 1914, Johnny's father leaves England to fight the Germans in France. With each carved wooden soldier he sends home, the brutality of war becomes more apparent. Soon Johnny fears that his war games foretell real battles and that he controls his father's fate.

Gathering Blue

Lois Lowry

0-440-22949-9

Lamed and suddenly orphaned, Kira is mysteriously taken to live in the palatial Council Edifice, where she is expected to use her gifts as a weaver to do the bidding of the all-powerful Guardians.

The Giver

Lois Lowry

0-440-23768-8

Jonas's world is perfect. Everything is under control. There is no war or fear or pain. There are no choices, until Jonas is given an opportunity that will change his world forever.

Shades of Simon Gray

Joyce McDonald

0-440-22804-2

Simon is the ideal teenager—smart, reliable, hardworking, trustworthy. Or is he? After Simon's car crashes into a tree and he slips into a coma, another portrait of him begins to emerge.

Harmony

Rita Murphy

0-440-22923-5

Power is coursing through Harmony—the power to affect the universe with her energy. This is a frightening gift for a girl who has always hated being different, and Harmony must decide whether to hide her abilities or embrace the consequences—good and bad—of her full strength.

Both Sides Now

Ruth Pennebaker

0-440-22933-2

A compelling look at breast cancer through the eyes of a mother and daughter. Liza must learn a few life lessons from her mother, Rebecca, about the power of family.

Her Father's Daughter

Mollie Poupeney

0-440-22879-4

As she matures from a feisty tomboy of seven to a spirited young woman of fourteen, Maggie discovers that the only constant in her life of endless new homes and new faces is her ever-emerging sense of herself.

The Baboon King

Anton Quintana

0-440-22907-3

Neither Morengáru's father's Masai tribe nor his mother's Kikuyu tribe accepts him. Banished from both tribes, Morengáru encounters a baboon troop and faces a fight with the simian king.

Holes

Louis Sachar

0-440-22859-X

Stanley has been unjustly sent to a boys' detention center, Camp Green Lake. But there's more than character improvement going on at the camp—the warden is looking for something.

Shabanu: Daughter of the Wind

Suzanne Fisher Staples

0-440-23856-0

Life is both sweet and cruel to strong-willed young Shabanu, whose home is the windswept Cholistan Desert of Pakistan. She must reconcile her duty to her family and the stirrings of her own heart in this Newbery Honor–winning modern-day classic.

The Gospel According to Larry

Janet Tashjian

0-440-23792-0

Josh Swensen's virtual alter ego, Larry, becomes a huge media sensation. While it seems as if the whole world is trying to figure out Larry's true identity, Josh feels trapped inside his own creation.

Memories of Summer

Ruth White

0-440-22921-9

In 1955, thirteen-year-old Lyric describes her older sister Summer's descent into mental illness, telling Summer's story with humor, courage, and love.